Death and the As

Phillip S

Copyright Page

Dedication

For Elli and Tais who both had the perseverance to make me sit down and write.

Chapter 1

Detective Inspector Keith Tremayne knew one thing: his idea of fun was not sitting on the grass on a balmy summer's night watching a rendition of Shakespeare's *Julius Caesar* acted out by the local dramatic society. He had to admit, though, that choosing the Anglo-Saxon fort of Old Sarum was as good a location as anywhere; not that much of it remained, just a few old stones here and there.

It had been six months since the events at nearby Avon Hill, and the village was supposedly half empty after ten of the men arrested were sent to prison for murder. The media had invaded the place for a few weeks after the revelations of pagan rituals and human sacrifices, but they had soon tired of it. Tremayne knew full well that what they really wanted was orgiastic rituals with a naked woman writhing in the centre of the old church while lecherous men ogled and took advantage. However, for worshippers of ancient gods, they had been a dreary group of people. There they were, a captive group of believers, and their idea of enjoyment was sacrificing some hapless individual whose only crime was believing in such nonsense.

Sitting there at Old Sarum, being bitten by mosquitoes and listening to amateur dramatics, was not the time to dwell on that case, especially as it was his sergeant's first week back at Bemerton Road Police Station, and he had agreed to accompany her to the play.

Personally, he would have preferred a quiet pint or two of beer, but Clare Yarwood, his sergeant, was definitely teetotal after the love of her life and her fiancé, Harry Holchester, the publican of the Deer's Head, his favourite pub, had turned out to be one of the elders of the pagan sect.

Tremayne could see that Yarwood was still not happy, even after several months of compassionate leave. He had never imagined that she would return, but there she had been several days earlier, standing in front of his desk on a Monday morning. 'Reporting for duty,' she had said.

It surprised him so much so that he had rushed round to her side of the desk and given her a big hug. The department had not been the same since she had left, and the only murder in the time she had been away, a wife of a butcher who had caught her husband in bed with her best friend. By the time she had finished with the two of them, they could have been served up in the man's shop, skilled as she was in preparing a cow or pig carcass for sale.

Tremayne looked up at the stage, looked at Yarwood. She looked fine, he thought, but he was still concerned. After all, she had seen the man she loved plucked from the ground and pinned in a tree, branches stabbing his body, even heard his last gasping breath. On the way to Old Sarum, she had asked him not to drive down Minster Street, so as not to see Harry's pub, closed since he had died.

For someone uncommonly disaffectionate, he had grown fond of her; she was almost like the daughter he had never had. And now, she was back in Salisbury, and there was no way that she could avoid painful memories being reactivated as they moved around the city.

On the stage, or in this case a rise in the ground, a man dressed in a Roman tunic made his speech:

Cowards die many times before their deaths; The valiant never taste of death but once. Of all the wonders that I yet have heard, it seems to me most strange that men should fear; Seeing that death, a necessary end, will come when it will come.

2

Tremayne wondered why the man didn't speak plain English, but then he was a blunt man, not used to beating around the bush, which was what the man was doing up on the stage. It was the last place that he'd ever visit of a night time, but he owed it to his sergeant to at least show interest in what she liked. It had been the two of them who had been intimately involved with the pagans, although others had come and gone in the Homicide department during the investigation, especially Vic Oldfield, the young and keen constable who fancied Clare but who had never had a chance while Harry was alive. And Oldfield had then died, along with a self-confessed murderer, in a crash on the Wilton Road.

Tremayne touched the crucifix around his neck at the thought of it. It was nonsense, this talk of ancient gods, and being able to summon them from the depths of wherever, but he had seen things he couldn't explain, the same as Yarwood. He would never admit it to her, nor even to himself, but it was weird at the time. The memory still remained of that night up in Cuthbert's Wood where the two of them, along with a couple of uniforms, had nearly been sacrificed in a pagan ritual.

If it hadn't been for Harry Holchester freeing Clare first, and then the others, all four would have died. Tremayne noticed that Yarwood still touched her ring finger. He knew that idling her time in the office would do her no good, but then idling her time back at her parent's hotel in Norfolk had got to her in the end; she'd admitted that to him.

What she needed, what they both needed, was a good juicy murder to take their minds off the past, not a group of actors prancing around in Roman attire. The only problem was that there weren't any murders on the boil at the present time, although after the medals had been dished out for bravery above and beyond the call of duty that night in Avon Hill, any talk by Superintendent Moulton of his forced retirement was definitely off the agenda.

He'd accepted the award on Yarwood's behalf, said a few words for her, but she had not wanted to come. It would have inevitably led to further discussion about her dead fiancé and Avon Hill, and she wasn't up to that, not even now.

***

Tremayne fidgeted where he sat, and cramp was starting to affect one leg. Any other time he would have run a mile from such an event, but he could see that Yarwood was engrossed. 'The good part is coming soon,' she said.

'Act 3, scene 1,' Tremayne said, which surprised him considering the violence in it. He had thought that after the events in Avon Hill and Harry's violent death, she'd not want to see any more.

'You've seen it before?'

'I went to school, you know. The English teacher was mad for Shakespeare. He made us read it through, and then a test to check that we had.'

'And had you?'

'Only to save one of his detentions, writing out one hundred times:

> *There is a tide in the affairs of men,*
> *Which, taken at the flood, leads on to fortune;*
> *Omitted, all the voyage of their life*
> *Is bound in shallows and in miseries.*
> *On such a full sea are we now afloat;*
> *And we must take the current when it serves,*
> *Or lose our ventures.*

It made no more sense then than it does now.'

'It's beautiful,' Yarwood replied.

'At least one of us is enjoying the night out.'

'The production and watching you squirm are poetic. Thanks for coming anyway. I knew it wasn't your kind of entertainment, but I didn't want to come on my own.'

'Don't expect me to come the next time, will you?'

'I'll be okay in a few days. It's just that coming back to Salisbury is not easy.'

'I'm pleased you're here.'

'You've missed me?' Yarwood asked.

'No one else could make a cup of tea like you,' Tremayne said. The friendliness between the two was making him uncomfortable. He had preferred it when he had snarled at her, and she had given him the occasional smart comment.

'You can make your own from now on. And besides, I prefer you grumpy.'

'Tomorrow, I promise. For tonight we'll labour through this.'

Tremayne had to admit that the production was professional, even if it was only the local dramatic society. He looked around: a full crowd. Amongst those watching were some in their teens, who seemed more engrossed than him. Also a fair smattering of retirees. He looked back at Yarwood.

'Don't worry about me. I'm made of stronger stuff,' Clare said. 'Harry's gone, life moves on, and I'm here.'

'I had you down as the whimpering type.'

'I was, but I've seen too much. I'd prefer him to be here, but he's not. It's no use dwelling on the past, is it?'

Tremayne had, that was the problem. The events in Avon Hill, the memories of his former wife, had made him phone her up. It had taken a few phone calls, a search on Facebook before he had traced her, and then it had been difficult.

They had met up: he, the set-in-his-ways detective inspector; she, the widowed mother of two.

'You look well,' she had said.

'So do you,' he had said, having to admit that she had fared better than him, but then, she hadn't spent nights in a pub drinking beer or working exhausting hours on murder investigations.

For a couple who had once been so close, it had been an uncomfortable night, too much water under the bridge. They had parted, a kiss on the cheek, not sure that they would meet up again, and Tremayne had to admit, he did like being on his own.

***

Tremayne was surprised that Yarwood would want to watch a production where there was to be a frenzied attack on the play's namesake, but for some reason it did not seem to affect her. As if the deaths of Harry, impaled by tree branches, and of an actor stabbed with fake retractable daggers and spilling red paint, were not similar.

He looked over at her as one of the major scenes in the play continued towards its crescendo. Up there on the stage were Caesar and the soothsayer.

CAESAR. *The ides of March are come.*

SOOTHSAYER. *Ay, Caesar; but not gone.*

Caesar, ignoring the advice, moving into the Senate and taking his seat. The plotting of Brutus and Cassius, the pleading of Metellus for his brother's banishment to end.

Is there no voice more worthy than my own
To sound more sweetly in great Caesar's ear
For the repeating of my banish'd brother?

Casca stabbing first, then the others, Cassius, Cinna, Ligarius, Metellus, Decius Brutus, and finally '*Et tu, Brute!*' as Brutus thrusts the final dagger in. Thirty-three times in total until the body lay at their feet.

Tremayne had to admit that it had been dramatic. The body of the actor covered in his robes, the blood oozing through, the conspirators with their bloodied hands, and then Brutus in the forum defending his and the conspirators' actions:

Be patient till the last.
Romans, countrymen, and lovers! hear me for my cause; and be
silent, that you may hear: believe me for mine honour, and have

respect to mine honour, that you may believe: censure me in your wisdom, and awake your senses, that you may the better judge. If there be any in this assembly, any dear friend of Caesar's, to him I say, that Brutus' love to Caesar was no less than his. If then that friend demand why Brutus rose against Caesar, this is my answer. Not that I loved Caesar less, but that I loved Rome more.

And then, the arrival of Caesar's body and the rebuke by Mark Antony:

Friends, Romans, countrymen, lend me your ears;
I come to bury Caesar, not to praise him.
The evil that men do lives after them;
The good is oft interred with their bones;
So let it be with Caesar. The noble Brutus
Hath told you Caesar was ambitious:
If it were so, it was a grievous fault, …

Finally, the body was taken away, to a hearty round of applause from the audience, even Tremayne. Yarwood was moved to tears. 'Are you alright?' Tremayne asked.

'The realism. I thought I could deal with it, but it made me remember.'

'Do you want to go?'

'No. I'll be fine. It's an intermission. I'll treat you to orange juice.'

'I could do with a beer.'

'After it's finished, we'll go to the Old Castle pub across the road,' Yarwood said. She had wanted to say the Deer's Head but corrected herself. That had been Harry's pub, the memory still painful of how he had saved her, how he had renounced the pagans up in Cuthbert's Wood and had come to her protection. She wanted to forget, but she could not.

***

'Tremayne, have you got a minute?'

Tremayne looked up from where he and Yarwood were sitting. 'Freestone, how are you? This is Sergeant Yarwood, Clare.'

'Pleased to meet you,' Clare said. She realised that he had been one of the actors on the stage, still dressed in his Roman tunic.

'It's around the back. We've called an ambulance and the police. I didn't realise you were here.'

'It's Yarwood. She's into this sort of thing.'

'At least one of you is not a philistine. Please come, it's serious.'

The two police officers got up from the grass and made their way around to the back of the stage, behind a cloth used as a backdrop.

'It's Gordon, he's dead.'

'Julius Caesar?' Clare said.

'They were meant to be fake knives. We'd purchased them especially.'

Tremayne knelt down, steadying himself on a chair to one side. He lifted the robe covering the man's face. 'You'll need to make an announcement.'

'That's what I was preparing to do. It has to be an accident, doesn't it?' Freestone said.

'That's not for me to say. Yarwood, make sure no one leaves until we've got their details and a brief statement.'

'The audience?'

'They may have seen something.'

Chapter 2

Peter Freestone handled the announcement reasonably well, Clare reinforcing his statement that the actor portraying Julius Caesar had unfortunately passed away.

There were one or two in the crowd who took the news badly, expecting a refund of their admission fee. They were more upset when told that no one was to leave until statements had been taken.

Tremayne didn't care whether they liked it or not. This was a murder, he was sure of it. He had been around long enough to know the difference between blood and red paint.

Clare was out front, trying to control the crowd, only one hundred and fifty or thereabouts. The sound of an ambulance could be heard as it hurtled up Castle Road towards the ancient site of Salisbury. Tremayne was around the back of the stage dealing with the cast. Freestone had returned to where the body was, leaving it to Clare and an employee of the Old Sarum Heritage Society to line up the people.

Already Clare had had to warn some of the more inebriated that leaving the scene of a crime was a criminal offence, even if they were not guilty of any wrongdoing.

The ambulance arrived, the medic rushing to examine the body of Gordon Mason, the actor who'd played Julius Caesar. 'I thought they used fake knives,' the medic, a petite woman, barely up to Tremayne's shoulder, said.

'I noticed the knife wounds. I'm assuming they killed him,' Tremayne said.

'That's not my area. I came here to save the man's life and to transport him to the hospital out on Odstock Road.'

'He'll need to go via Pathology first.'

'I take it you want me to leave the body where it is for your crime scene people.'

'You know the routine?'

'Once or twice. And besides, the man is dead. There's not much I can do.'

Jim Hughes, the crime scene examiner, the man that Tremayne begrudgingly had to admit was competent, even if he was still on the young side, arrived. As Yarwood had told him on more than one occasion, Hughes was degree educated, as if that somehow helped. Tremayne knew that he was a cantankerous sod, always pushing those who did not push back, and Hughes had given as much as he'd taken.

As far as Tremayne was concerned, strong-willed, competent, willing to challenge him with rational argument and a little sarcasm were plus points, and Yarwood was fast becoming the master, or should it be mistress, he wasn't sure which of the two was politically correct. Not that he had a lot of time for those who expounded the virtues of talking nicely to one another, showing due deference. If the person was a villain, enquiring after their health wasn't going to help, but a kick up the rear end and a few firm words, expletives included, would do more good.

'What do you reckon?' Tremayne asked one minute after Hughes had commenced his examination of Gordon Mason.

'He wouldn't have lasted long as King anyway.'

'You've lost me there.'

'Didn't you read the synopsis?'

'Yarwood did. She gave me the gist,' Tremayne said. He knew the plot as well as any of them, having had it drummed into him at school, but playing the uncouth policeman, ignorant of anything other than the racing results and a police report, maintained the image he wanted to portray.

'Cassius convinced Brutus that Caesar was attempting to be the King of Rome, do away with the Senate. That's why they killed him.'

'As you were saying about Mason?'

'Heavy smoker, overweight, and certainly no exercise judging by the tone of his muscles.'

'You can tell all that by looking at him lying there?'

'Not at all. Mason dealt with the purchase of our house. He was a solicitor, competent as far as we're concerned.'

'How many knife wounds?'

'Daggers.'

'Daggers, knives, what's the difference?'

'In this case, not a lot. I can see that the body's been pierced in several places.'

'They stabbed him at least thirty times on the stage.'

'Did you count?'

'No, but it's thirty-three according to Shakespeare.'

'You read that in the programme?'

'Yes, that's it,' Tremayne said. He had almost slipped up; almost revealed a hitherto hidden area of his knowledge.

'There's not that many stab wounds, maybe four or five. There's a couple in the area of the heart, two or three on the body. Pathology will be more precise, but I'd say that just one or two of them were fatal. The daggers? Are they here?'

'I have them.'

'How many?'

'Seven.'

'Okay, that's the right number. Any chance of fingerprints?'

'It's possible, but they've got lacquered rope on the handles, wooden pommels.'

'Are the daggers safe?'

'They're all in the same area,' Tremayne said. 'I've already shown one of your team where they are.'

'And the actors from the scene?'

'They're out the front.'

'We'll get their fingerprints first, and then see if we can get a match.'

Hughes concluded his preliminary examination of the body. He and Tremayne walked around the area. 'He was there when he was stabbed,' Tremayne said, pointing to a rise in the ground.

'Where Caesar was assassinated,' Hughes corrected him.

'He doesn't look much of a Caesar back there, does he?'

'You're right. What else do we have?'

'The other actors, although your people are dealing with them,' Tremayne said. 'The only thing that confuses me is how they came to be using real daggers. I thought they always used fake knives, plastic blades, blades that retracted inside the handles when they were pressed against a hard surface.'

'That's what we'll need to find out. One other thing, whoever killed Gordon Mason would have known that his dagger was entering the body.'

'Are you certain?'

'I'll confirm it once Forensics has checked the daggers, but yes, I'm certain. It's one thing to push a blade into a body, another to jab, the blade retracting.'

'One of the actors?'

'I found four to five wounds. It's one, maybe two actors.'

'And the other actors? Wouldn't they have realised that something was amiss?'

'You'd think so, but they may have been focussing on their part, their lines.'

'In that case, the murderer or murderers must have known which daggers to pick up. I never saw any markings to separate them.'

'There'll be something. I'll get them checked, let you know.'

Tremayne, an admirable man in many ways, had difficulty in accepting people unproven, but Hughes had won the blunt DI's respect in their previous case in Avon Hill, as had his sergeant, Clare Yarwood. Tremayne walked over to her. 'Okay, Yarwood?' he said.

'I'm just getting the details of the actors. Some of them are upset.'

'Not all of them,' Tremayne replied.

'It's not an accident, a faulty prop?'

'One, maybe two, of our thespians here is a murderer, and he or they know it.'

'They'll not admit to it, not up here tonight.'

'If they can pretend to be someone else on a stage, I'm sure they can maintain the pretence of being innocent.'

'The uniforms are taking the names and addresses of the audience, taking brief statements, but they're unlikely to have seen anything.'

'The same as us. We were out front, and we didn't see it, and we're trained to observe,' Tremayne said.

'Can I tell the actors that Julius Caesar was murdered? Most of them think it was an accident. They keep telling me what a great guy Gordon Mason was.'

'And a good solicitor no doubt.'

'They didn't mention that.'

'Hughes did. I'll tell them the truth. You watch for their reactions.'

'Ladies and gentlemen, I'm Detective Inspector Tremayne. I'll be leading this investigation.'

'We're all upset. We'd like to go home,' a woman said.

'And you are?' Tremayne said.

'Fiona Dowling. I played Calpurnia.'

Clare leaned over towards her boss and whispered, 'Caesar's wife.'

'Yarwood, I don't need a lesson on Shakespeare. I'm not the fool you take me for.'

'Sorry, guv.'

'Miss Dowling?'

'Mrs.'

'Mrs Dowling, I'm afraid it's not that simple. Gordon Mason was murdered.'

'But why? How?' one of the men asked.

'And you are?'

'Trevor Winston. I played Casca,' a slightly built, effeminate man said.

'The first assassin,' Tremayne said.

Clare looked at her DI in bewilderment. A man with no interest in anything outside of the police station, save for horse racing and pints of beer, and yet here was a man who knew his Shakespeare.

'One or two of the daggers were either tampered with or exchanged for real daggers. Forensics will tell us in due course. In the meantime, all of the conspirators must remain suspects.'

'But how would we know that the dagger was real? I'm Geoff Pearson, Cassius.'

'Mr Pearson, the difference between stabbing a man with a fake dagger and a real one is noticeable. Unfortunately, one or two of you here, or should I say of the men, is a murderer.'

'It can't be,' another woman said.

'Your name?'

'Cheryl Milledge. I played Portia.'

'Brutus's wife,' Tremayne said.

'You know your Shakespeare.'

'I know what they drummed into me at school.'

Clare realised that Tremayne may pretend that he was a simple man with few interests, but he was, in fact, more knowledgeable that he was willing to admit. She also realised that it was the first time that she had not thought about the events at Avon Hill when Harry had died.

'As I was saying,' Tremayne repeated, 'one, possibly two, of the seven men who stabbed Gordon Mason here tonight is a murderer. We don't know which of you it is, but we will in due course.'

Clare spent another forty minutes dealing with the actors before returning to the other side of the makeshift stage.

'Any reaction?' Tremayne asked.

'Apart from them all profusely protesting their innocence?'

'*Methinks thou dost protest too much,*' Tremayne said. 'Hamlet, by the way. It's not the correct quotation, but it's the one people remember.'

'You've been studying while I've been away,' Clare said.

'Don't get ahead of yourself, Yarwood. Just because I remember a few lines of Shakespeare, it doesn't mean I'm not the same cranky bastard that you know.'

'I won't, guv.'

'After I told them that one or two of them was a murderer?'

'A look of shock from all of them, nothing more.'

'You'd never know with them, trained to cover their true feelings.'

'They're the local drama society, they're hardly the Royal Shakespeare Company. I doubt if they're that good.'

'Maybe, but it's not important. We'll wait for Hughes's report before our next move.'

'You're not holding the seven?'

'We know where they are. Let them go. And besides, I could do with a beer.'

'Too late, guv. The pubs are all closed.'

Tremayne looked at his watch; it was close to midnight. 'Hell, Yarwood. Shakespeare, murder, and not even a pint. What a way to spend an evening.'

Tomorrow, I'll treat you,' Clare said.

'You know what will happen?'

'Another murder, more evidence, longer hours in the office and on the road.'

'And less time for a beer. I was hoping to go to the races this Saturday. I can guarantee I won't be.'

'For me, I'd rather be busy.'

'At least one of us is pleased,' Tremayne said.

Clare knew that, regardless of his protestations, the man was pleased as well, and this case had intrigue, the sort of case that her DI, even she, liked.

Chapter 3

Clare hadn't slept that first few nights back in Salisbury. She had leased a small cottage in Stratford sub Castle, not far from where Mavis Godwin, another victim of the pagan murderer, had lived. Her return to the city with its unpleasant memories had not been easy, but being back home with her parents, well-meaning but always trying to organise her life, convince her to take over as the manager of their hotel, had not been easy either. And besides, Salisbury had been where she had felt some contentment until that awful night when she had nearly died, and Harry, her fiancé, had. She had hoped to avoid the memories of him, the places they had visited together, but she knew that would not be possible, and now she wasn't sure if she wanted to.

He had turned out to be bad, but in the end he had saved her life at the expense of his. Tremayne would not agree, but he had not loved the man, she had, and her memories of Harry Holchester would only be good ones. He had been buried in the graveyard at Avon Hill, the church re-consecrated with a new vicar. Clare knew that she wanted to go out there, place some flowers on the grave, but she was not ready yet.

At seven in the morning after the play, she was in the office at Bemerton Road Police Station. She could see that Tremayne was all the better for a night without beer, but then, the man always looked better when he had a murder case.

'You're looking smart, guv,' Clare said.

'Don't think it's because of you,' the standard gruff reply. Clare had missed his abrasive manner, his self-deprecating comments, even their repartee. With her parents, sticklers for good manners, dressing for dinner, it had become boring, but with Tremayne, his shirt sometimes unironed, his tie off to one side, his attempts at picking the horses, she felt a homeliness in his company.

'I didn't think it was, guv.'

'And besides, you look smart enough for the two of us.'

'What's the plan for today?' Clare asked.

'Unless Jim Hughes comes up with something, which I don't think he will, you and I are out on the road interviewing the seven assassins.'

'You don't have much hope with Forensics?'

'I hope we get something, but all the daggers were identical, visually that is.'

'But there must have been a difference.'

'There has to be, but they had been thrown on a table at the rear after the scene. I'm certain that other people came along afterwards and moved them. There's bound to be plenty of fingerprints, but it'll be difficult to find one set that identifies the murderer.'

'Who do you believe is the most likely assassin?' Clare asked.

'Murderer, you mean.'

'Yes, murderer.'

'What do we know about Act 3, Scene 1?'

'The assassination?'

'Yes.'

'Seven assassins, the first stab from Casca, then the others join in. The final stab from Brutus.'

'Et tu, Brute.'

'Brutus only stabs Caesar once, but Jim Hughes said there were four or five stab wounds,' Clare said.

'In that case, Peter Freestone, he played Brutus, is not guilty on his own.'

★

'No luck,' Hughes said, in Tremayne's office.

'What do you mean?' Tremayne asked. It was apparent that Hughes and his team, together with Forensics, had worked all night, as it was only eight thirty in the morning, and they had a report prepared.

'Two of the daggers had been tampered with.'

'What do you mean?'

'It was clever. The retracting mechanism would work, but someone had drilled a small hole through the handle on each one. It's not easy to see, but once we examined them under a bright light, we could see it.'

'Are you saying that they were all dangerous?'

'Only the two.'

'Someone had taken them and fitted metal blades?'

'It's very clever. Those that retracted did no harm; the murder weapons when pressed hard did.'

'So afterwards, it would have been possible to identify which blade killed the man.'

'They were covered in blood or red paint up at Old Sarum. There was no way to tell up there.'

'Fingerprints?'

'Inconclusive.'

'How many of the daggers had real blood on them?'

'Most of them, as they had all stabbed the body a few times. They would have picked up at least some blood on the outside of the man's robe. What I can tell you is that you have two murderers. Those daggers that had entered the body had substantially more blood than the others, consistent with entry through the flesh.'

'Anything more?'

'Pathology will conduct the autopsy. They'll be able to tell you the extent of the wounds, and which of the daggers killed the man, but you've still got two potential murderers.'

***

'Dreadful business, Tremayne,' Peter Freestone said. The man, someone that Tremayne occasionally drank with, was in his office in Salisbury, perilously close to Minster Street and Harry Holchester's pub. Tremayne, sensitive to his sergeant's fragile nature, had attempted to deviate around the area, distracting her as they drove past the end of the road. It had not been successful as she had looked, seen the pub sign hanging over the door, not that there would be much of a welcome, closed as it had been for some months. There had been a couple of offers since to buy the place, but none had come to anything.

Freestone sat in his office at the far end of Guildhall Square. Tremayne thought the room had a warm and cosy feel; Clare did not like it. Freestone, an accountant, was successful by all accounts, in that he lived well, had a big house not far from Salisbury, drove a late model Mercedes, and smoked a pipe in the office.

Tremayne liked the idea of the pipe, Clare did not, the smell permeating the office. 'Sorry about the smell,' Freestone said as he opened the window.

'It's fine by me,' Tremayne said. 'Okay by you, Yarwood?'

'Fine,' Clare replied, which it was not, but they were there to discuss a murder, not to debate the offensive smell.

'None of us slept last night,' Freestone said.

'Did anyone admit to killing the man?'

'I can't believe that one of us killed him.'

'Someone did,' Clare said.

'But why? We act for the love of theatre, not for an opportunity to commit murder.'

'That's as maybe,' Tremayne said, 'but some of your group killed the man.'

'Some?'

'There were seven in that assassination scene, seven who stabbed Gordon Mason. Two of you had lethal weapons.'

'But how?'

'We know how. We still don't know who. What can you tell us about the other six?'

'I was Brutus. Then there's Casca, Cassius, Cinna, Ligarius, Metellus, and Decius Brutus.'

'Maybe you can start with Casca?' Clare asked.

'Trevor Winston. He has a hairdressing salon. He would like to act professionally, but he's not good enough. He knows that, so I'm not talking out of turn.'

'Anything else?'

'He's effeminate.'

'Gay?'

'He tries to downplay it, but yes, he probably is. He wouldn't harm a fly.'

'We're not dealing with flies here,' Tremayne said.

'You know what I mean.'

'Of course. I'm sure they are all fine, upstanding people, but two wanted Gordon Mason dead. Any ideas as to why?'

'Not that I know of. The man was competent, active in the dramatic society. He could be blunt sometimes, especially with Trevor Winston.'

'Any reason why?'

'Mason was a strict Baptist. He didn't hold with homosexuals.'

'Reason enough for Winston to bear a grudge?' Tremayne asked.

'I wouldn't have thought so. They tolerated each other, worked well together on stage, and besides, Winston's harmless.'

'You've already said that.'

'Apologies. Who else do you want to know about?'

'The assassins.'

'Cassius, the villain of the piece.'

'Why do you say that?' Clare asked.

'I thought you knew your Shakespeare,' Tremayne said. Clare ignored his barbed comment. She much preferred the philistine to the educated man that her DI had temporarily become.

'Cassius was the one who convinced Brutus that Caesar wanted to wrest control from the Senate and to pronounce himself King,' Freestone said.

'Who played that part?' Tremayne asked.

'Geoff Pearson, an archaeology student, very bright, talented actor.'

'Local, is he?'

'Born and bred. He's studying at the university in Southampton, drives there and back every day.'

'Any aggravation with anyone else in the cast?' Clare asked.

'Not Geoff. He gets on well with everyone.'

'Cinna, what about him?' Tremayne asked.

'Gary Barker.'

'Profession, age?'

'He's an easy-going person, mid-thirties, not very ambitious. He's a good actor though. Cheryl Milledge, his girlfriend, played Portia, Brutus's wife. She likes to drink, so does Gary.'

'Decius Brutus?'

'Len Dowling. You must have seen his signs around the city.'

'The estate agent?'

'I thought I recognised him,' Tremayne said. 'He gave me a lousy valuation on my house a couple of years back. He was desperate to sell it for me.'

'Did you?'

'No way. He showed me what I could buy instead. I was better off where I am, and besides, I like it where I live. Apart from him being a sharp operator, what more can you tell us about him?'

'He's very keen on the theatrical. He's a competent actor, agreeable with everyone, although he can be overbearing. His wife, Fiona, played Calpurnia, the wife of Caesar.'

'Is Dowling capable of murder?' Tremayne asked.

'How would I know?' Freestone replied. 'How does anyone know if someone else is capable of murder?'

'Metellus, what about him?'

'Bill Ford. He's a funeral director. He's not an affable man, but yet again, enthusiastic. Always puts in a good performance. He keeps to himself, lives on his own.'

'Gay?'

'Unlikely. I can't see him being close to anyone, male or female. He comes to our rehearsals, knows his lines, and he'll always be here on the night. Apart from that, I can't tell you much more about him.'

'Apart from you, that only leaves Ligarius,' Tremayne said.

'Jimmy Francombe. He's only young, no more than eighteen. He's exceptionally keen, impetuous, always wanting to hog the limelight, reckons he's better than the parts we give him.'

'Is he?'

'Probably, but he needs to mature. Sometimes, he'll turn up with a throbbing headache and a hangover after a night on the town. We can't trust him with the major parts until he grows out of it.'

'What about Mark Antony?'

'Phillip Dennison.'

'Friends, Romans and countrymen,' Tremayne said.

'Yes, that's it. Dennison, wealthy, thinks he's superior to all of us, but he's reliable, and he enjoys acting. His wife's a handful.'

'Any reason why you say that?'

'You'll judge for yourself when you meet them. Phillip's in his late fifties, his wife's twenty to twenty-five years younger, trophy wife.'

'Is she? Clare asked.

'I might be wrong, but that's how I see it. Mind you, she's beautiful. I can't blame the man. That's the cast for the scene, apart from me. I played Brutus. I only stabbed Gordon once.'

'A clear target to the heart, though,' Tremayne said.

'Not me. I had nothing against Mason. He could be a killjoy, orange juice at the pub, but apart from that he was a good solicitor, used him myself on more than a few occasions.'

***

Tremayne and Clare left Freestone to his pipe and his spreadsheets. They walked across Guildhall Square, Tremayne aiming to walk in one direction, Clare walking in the other.

'Are you ready for this?' Tremayne asked.

'I doubt if I'll ever be ready, but I can't be in Salisbury and do my job if you keep driving down other streets, trying to avoid Harry's pub.'

'It's still raw?'

'It's better here, and now we've got another murder to deal with. I'll be better, believe me.'

Tremayne was not sure; his sergeant still looked emotionally disturbed to him, although he could not blame her. He had liked Harry Holchester, always thought him to be a decent person, and he had been equally surprised when he had turned out to be one of the pagan worshippers.

The two police officers rounded the corner. There, in front of them, the Deer's Head, the pub where Tremayne had often enjoyed a pint, where Clare had first met Harry. Tremayne, a man who rarely showed emotion, let alone felt it, looked at Clare.

'I shouldn't have come,' she said.

Tremayne felt sad for her. 'We've got work to do,' he said.

'Give me a few minutes on my own.'

Tremayne walked away, took out a cigarette and lit up. He kept a watch on his sergeant, saw that she was just standing there, not moving, not crying. She reminded him of a porcelain statue. He didn't know why he had made that analogy; he wasn't a man who delved too deeply into the romanticism of a moment, but for some reason, he did that day.

Clare looked over at him. 'I'm fine now. I just had to deal with the rush of emotions. In future, if driving down past Harry's pub is the quickest way, then we drive down there. No more diverting up this road and down that. Clear?'

'And from here on, no more inviting me to watch boring plays. Clear?'

'There's still a murder to deal with,' Clare said.

'We need to interview the others.'

Chapter 4

Tremayne did not like Len Dowling, having met him before. To him, the man was too brash, too pushy, and above all, intent on distorting the truth, telling a vendor their house was worth more than it was, telling a purchaser that it was a bargain.

That was what had happened to him when he had let the man show him a few houses. On the one hand, he was there attempting to convince him that it was a steal, the owner desperate, and with a little bit of TLC he'd clean up financially on this one, and then with the vendor, singing another tune.

Tremayne remembered when he had allowed Dowling to show a young couple around his house in Wilton. The estate agent was priming him to expect an imminent offer, and then Tremayne had overheard him telling the young couple that the owner was desperate to sell: financial difficulties. As far as he was concerned, the man they were going to talk to was guilty of crimes against decency. It was not the ideal situation, Tremayne realised, to harbour prejudices.

'Sorry, busy day,' Dowling said. For a man with so much energy, he did not look healthy. His skin was pallid, his weight was on the heavy side. He wore a suit with a red tie, although even Tremayne had to admit he wore it well, handmade probably, whereas Tremayne was strictly an off-the-rack sort of man.

'We've some questions,' Clare said.

'In my office,' Dowling said.

Inside were the pictures of houses sold, the advertising leaflets on the floor, the awards on his desk. 'Business good?' Tremayne asked.

'Booming market, interest rates are low. It's never been a better time to buy.'

'Or sell?'

'I remember your place. I could get you a good price.'

'We're here to discuss a murder, not my house.'

'Understood. I get wound up sometimes. We never slept last night, Fiona and I.'

'Calpurnia.'

Tremayne knew that Dowling was not a man who would have any trouble sleeping.

'You played Decius Brutus?' Clare said.

'I wanted to play Caesar.'

'Any reason?'

'Fiona was playing his wife. I thought it would be fun, great for the business.'

'Why?'

'I'd ensure an article in the paper. Local estate agent and his wife take leading roles in Shakespeare's *Julius Caesar*.'

'Instead of a local estate agent takes a minor role, while his wife gets the plum female part.'

'You've got it,' Dowling said. Clare thought the man was awful, the same as her DI, judging by the way he looked at the estate agent.

'Caesar died,' Tremayne said.

'In the play.'

'Outside of the play as well.'

'Yes, but that was Mason, not Caesar.'

'Was it? What if someone wanted to make a statement, or they were jealous that they did not get the part?'

'Whoa. Are you accusing me of murder just because I didn't get to play the lead?'

'People murder each other for the strangest of reasons, jealousy is as good as any.'

'It wasn't that important. Granted that Gordon Mason wasn't the most jovial of men, but a part in the local dramatic society's production is hardly a reason to kill him.'

'What would be?'

'He was a good solicitor.'

'Don't tell me that you use him as well.'

Clare could see that Tremayne was baiting the man, attempting to get past his supercilious grin.'

'I've never used him. My brother is a solicitor in Salisbury.'

'What would be a good enough reason to kill Mason?' Tremayne asked.

'Can there be any?'

'You've got your finger on the pulse of what goes on in this city. Any rumours of suspect property transactions, criminal activities?'

'There's always rumours, but nothing specific, and besides, Gordon Mason was a strict Bible-bashing Baptist. He's hardly likely to be the type of person to be involved in anything criminal.'

'Dodgy property transactions, rezoning industrial into residential, may not be illegal, only fraudulent. Are there any such activities?'

'Not that I know of.'

'You'd tell us if you knew?'

'Inspector, I gild the lily, portray myself as Jack the lad, everyone's friend, but basically, I'm a decent person. Mason may have been involved in shady deals, he may have been obstructing some, but I don't know any more than you do. I can't say that I'll miss the man. I didn't know him that well, and maybe I'll get a crack at Caesar next time, but I didn't kill him, and I don't know who did.'

'Thanks. You've answered our questions,' Tremayne said.

'Have I?'

'You gave an honest reply. Murderers invariably defend themselves by effusing excessively about the victim, a great loss to society, loved his wife, loved animals.'

'He'll not be missed much,' Dowling said. 'Now can I get back to what I do best?'

'Of course.'

Tremayne and Clare left Dowling's agency, the man back into ingratiating mode – it's a bargain, we'll get you a good price – with an elderly couple who had walked in the door.

'They'll see through him soon enough,' Tremayne said.

'Will they?' Clare said.

'Not really my concern.'

***

'Yarwood, you can deal with Jimmy Francombe. He'll open up more with you,' Tremayne said.

The two had just had a break, discussed Len Dowling. Both agreed that the man was a typical salesman, but it was hardly a reason to become a murderer.

'Why me?' Clare said.

'You're more his age. He'll clam up with me.'

'What do you mean? He'll see me as a bit of fluff, attempt to chat me up.'

'Yarwood, you know I didn't say that. You're getting touchy. What I meant to say is that he'll see me as an old man, more like a father figure. With you, he'll see you as his age. No doubt he'll fancy you, what young hot-blooded male wouldn't, but that's not the reason.'

'Thanks,' Clare said. 'You know how to compliment people.'

'That wasn't a compliment.'

'It was to me.'

'Anyway, you deal with Francombe.'

Clare found Jimmy Francombe at his school. As it was a murder investigation, she had contacted their administration department, who had pulled him out of his class.

'I've a few questions,' Clare said, once they were sitting in a small office at the school.

'I saw you up at Old Sarum. Did you see me?'

'On the stage and when I took your statement.'

'I'm better than them.'

Clare could see that the young man, who looked older than eighteen, more like twenty-two to twenty-four, had the arrogance of youth, the infallibility of the young, and the raging hormones of an adolescent teenager.

'You played Ligarius?'

'I didn't kill him.'

27

'Caesar or Gordon Mason.'

'Both.'

'What can you tell me about the death scene?'

'It was as we had rehearsed it. Casca, that's Trevor Winston, he stabbed Caesar first.'

'Do you like Trevor Winston?'

'He's not a bad person; he's gay.'

'Has he tried it on with you?'

'He knows I'd give him a thump if he tried it.'

'Are you violent?'

'Not me. With Trevor, it's a few laughs, make a few gay jokes, but the man likes a drink occasionally. I see him around the city with his gay friends sometimes, that's all.'

'After Casca?'

'Do you know the story?' Francombe asked. Clare could see that he was looking her up and down. She was not much older than him, and with her fresh-faced look and his mature, slightly-lined face, complete with a two-day stubble, they looked as if they could have made a couple, not that she was interested in younger men, or men in general, at the present time. And she resented his piercing eyes. She regretted that she had worn a white blouse that day, see-through if the sun was shining in the right direction.

'Jimmy, do me a favour.'

'What is it?'

'Stop eyeing me up and down. I'm here as a police sergeant investigating a murder.'

'You should have sent the old man.'

'The old man, as you refer to him, is a detective inspector, a very experienced police officer.'

'I'm sorry,' Francombe said, 'I'll be on my best behaviour from now on.'

Clare's impression of the youth changed. He seemed to be a pleasant person, even if a little immature. She understood the reluctance of the dramatic society to rely on him for more significant roles.

'According to Peter Freestone, you're a good actor.'

'I know, I know. When I grow up.'

'Something like that. Jimmy, swap seats.'

'Sorry.'

'You've said that already.'

'You're a good sort. Has anyone told you that before?'

'No, you're the first,' Clare said with a smile.

The two of them changed seats. Clare was now in shadow.

'As I was saying, do you know the plot?'

'Yes.'

'After Casca, the other conspirators come forward and start stabbing Caesar. And finally, the 'Et tu, Brute' where Brutus plunges the final dagger in.'

'When you used your dagger, did it feel unusual?'

'Do you mean if it felt as if I was using a real dagger?'

'Yes.'

'It felt the same as we had practised.'

'How many times did you stab?'

'Three, maybe four.'

'You can't be sure?'

'I'm fairly certain it was three, but there's not a lot of room up on the stage with six of us attempting to stab Caesar, and I wasn't counting.'

'Are you certain your knife was retracting?'

'I thought it was. I'm not certain if I'd know.'

'Thank you. I've no further questions for now.'

Francombe stood up. 'My mates are going to ask questions. They saw me come in here with you.'

'Tell them you've set up a hot date for the weekend.'

'Have I?'

'Not a chance.'

'I thought not. I'm sorry about what happened.'

'At Old Sarum?'

'No. Before.'

'Avon Hill?'

'I was friends with Adam Saunders.'

'He didn't deserve to die.'

'Nor did the other man, the one you were keen on.'

'No, I suppose he didn't, but that's life. It's not all a bed of roses.'

'Are you sure the hot date is off?'

'Certain. Thanks for your assistance.'

'I'm going to brag about this, you know that?'

'Brag on, that's all you've got.'

'Holchester was a lucky man.'

'It's in the past.'

'Sorry, I've brought up unpleasant memories.'

'Please leave. You've plenty of bragging to do.'

Jimmy Francombe left. Clare took out a handkerchief and cried. After five minutes, she left, remembering to wave at Jimmy as he bragged to his mates.

***

Clare returned to Bemerton Road. She found Tremayne in his office, in deep thought. 'What's up, guv?' she asked.

'I'm just thinking through what we saw on the stage. Apart from the melee of the actors stabbing Mason, was there anything else?'

'Such as?'

'Is it possible to make any assumptions as to which of the assassins was stabbing harder. I'm assuming that someone with a fake knife is going for effect, not intending to hurt the man.'

'You're right. Even a fake knife would hurt if pushed hard against a body, whereas the murderer would not be concerned.'

'There'd be bruising. Fancy a trip to Pathology. They're conducting the autopsy today. Have you ever seen one?'

'Not me.'

'Come on. It's good experience,' Tremayne said.

Clare was well aware of the procedure, the slicing open of the body, the removal of all the vital organs, the extraction of the brain, the attempt afterwards to make it palatable for the family to see their loved one.

Tremayne and Yarwood found the pathologist in his office, the examination of Gordon Mason completed. Tremayne appeared to be disappointed, Clare was not.

'What do you want to know, Tremayne?' Dr Stuart Collins, the forensic pathologist, asked. Clare had met him before.

'Gordon Mason. Do you have a report?'

'I'm typing it up.'

Clare knew the pathologist to be a precise man, not willing to give much away until the report was complete. Tremayne, she knew, was the opposite: wanting to get on with the investigation, not appreciative of delays.

'We've a few questions,' Tremayne said.

'You'll not go away until I've given you something, will you?'

'You know how it is.'

'With you, Tremayne, I do. What is it?'

Clare could see that the two men had a good relationship.

'The man was stabbed thirty-three times,' Tremayne said.

'Thirty-four,' Collins replied.

'One extra,' Clare said.

'Shakespeare may be rolling over in his grave that someone deviated from the script, but it was thirty-four.'

'How many penetrated the skin?'

'Five. One in the liver, another in a kidney, one a minor wound, and two to the heart.'

'The heart wound's fatal?'

'I'll detail it in my report, but yes, both of the wounds in the heart would have been fatal. The other wounds in the body would have caused severe bleeding, but the man would have been conscious long enough for an ambulance to arrive and administer emergency treatment.'

'After the wounds to the heart, how long would he have lived?'

'He'd have been in shock within a minute, possibly less. He would have died soon after. There's still some final analysis on the heart as to whether it was the left or right ventricle. I'll be more precise in the final report.'

'One other question,' Tremayne said.

'I'm a busy man.'

'We all are.'

'What is it?'

'Can you tell how many times the area around the man's heart was impacted by a dagger, retractable or not.'

'There's slight bruising from the retractable daggers. The man should have been wearing a specially-designed padded vest, but apparently he was wearing a camping jacket under his robe.'

'How many daggers to the heart?'

'Four. Two pierced the skin, two did not. Any more questions?'

'Of the daggers that pierced the heart and the body, can you tell how many there were?'

'We found irregularities in the wounds which would indicate two different blades.'

'Thanks. That agrees with Jim Hughes's analysis.'

***

'You look as though you could do with your roots being dealt with,' Tremayne said outside the pathologist's office.

'Is that a criticism or your way of saying that we should visit Trevor Winston?'

'Just my attempt at humour.'

'A feeble attempt.'

Trevor Winston was not difficult to spot in his hairdressing salon on New Canal Street. At Old Sarum, he had been dressed in a Roman tunic, the same as all the other assassins, but in his shop the man wore bright yellow trousers, a white shirt open almost to the waist. He was welcoming to the two police officers as they came in.

'They're going to arrest me for your hairstyles,' Winston joked with his customers.

In the backroom, Winston apologised. 'Sorry about that. They expect me to be over the top, a younger version of Kenneth Williams. You remember him, I'm sure.'

'I do,' Tremayne said.

'Vaguely,' Clare said.

'Are you? Tremayne asked. 'Gay, that is?'

'If you mean homosexual, then yes, I am. We're not all over the top though. Outside of the salon, you'd not pick me from any other man in the street.'

'Gordon Mason did.'

'The man was a bore. He didn't like anyone who wasn't like him.'

'Baptist, teetotal?'

'Repressed,' Winston said.

'Was he?'

'I'd say so. Gordon was friendly with Peter Freestone and Bill Ford. Both of them had boring professions.'

'An accountant and a funeral director,' Clare said.

'I like Bill Ford,' Winston said. 'He takes himself seriously, the profession I suppose, but he's easy enough to get on with.'

'Peter Freestone?' Tremayne asked.

'He likes to take control, he was the director of this production, but he's okay. At least he'll have a pint with you at the end of the day.'

'What about the other cast members?'

'Jimmy Francombe, he's only young, but he's a good actor. Len Dowling and his wife, Fiona. I don't mind them, although Len is up himself.'

'Up himself?' Tremayne asked.

'Thinks he's better than he is,' Clare said.

'We'd agree with you on that,' Tremayne said.

'Who else?' Winston thought out loud. 'Gary Barker, he's keen. Not much of a conversationalist. And then there's his girlfriend, Cheryl Milledge.'

'What about her?' Clare asked.

'I've known her a few years, the town bike back then.'

'You don't want that explaining, do you, guv?' Clare asked.

'I know what he means.'

'They've both settled down now, but she can drink like a fish. Gary tries to stop her, but he's wasting his time.'

'Tough woman?'

'With Gary. They're both keen on acting.'

'You didn't like Gordon Mason?' Tremayne asked.

'He didn't like me, but I had no real problem with him. We both enjoyed acting, and we could work together. Outside of acting, he'd ignore me in the street.'

'Peter Freestone said that you had regarded acting as a vocation.'

'I would have loved to do it, but I'm not up to the leading man status, and the money's dreadful if you're not on top. I make a lot more here, and I'm content with that.'

'Anyone you would suspect of wanting Gordon Mason dead?'

'He was a gruff man, but dead? I don't think so, but then I didn't know him very well.'

'Anyone who would have?'

'As I said, Peter Freestone and Bill Ford.'

Chapter 5

After the flamboyant Trevor Winston, Bill Ford came as something of a revelation. One had looked like an advert for high-definition television with his vivid colours, the other like a flashback to the days of black and white.

Clare half-expected the man to put on a top hat, as she had seen in English horror movies from the sixties. However, apart from his sombre appearance, he was polite, even if rather direct.

'What can you tell us about the events of last night?' Tremayne asked. The three of them were standing in a back room of the funeral director's premises, where several coffins were lined up ready for use.

'Excuse the surroundings. It's a busy day.'

'Gordon Mason?'

'I've been contracted to deal with him.'

'His body's not been released yet.'

'That's understood,' Ford said. Clare thought he smelt of formaldehyde.

'You took the part of Metellus?' Tremayne asked.

'I was the one pleading with Caesar:

Is there no voice more worthy than my own?
To sound more sweetly in great Caesar's ear
For the repealing of my banish'd brother?

Tremayne did not need another recital. Clare thought it attractive to see a funeral director dressed in black reciting his lines.

'You were there when Gordon Mason was stabbed?'

'I was integral to the scene. I must have stabbed him at least twice.'

'Nobody seems firm on the numbers,' Tremayne said.

35

'It's always frenetic. There's six of us crowded around Caesar, lunging forward, pulling back, aiming to get out of the way of the others.'

'Is that all?'

'Not really. We're all trying to make it look realistic, attempting not to let the audience see the daggers retracting.'

'Did yours?'

'No question on that.'

'According to our reports, it's not so easy to tell if the dagger is entering the body or not.' Tremayne knew that he had made up the statement to judge the man's response.

'I'm a funeral director. I know what it feels like to insert a knife into sinew and gut. My dagger retracted, I'm sure of it.'

'Is there anyone who may have had a grudge against Gordon Mason?'

'Not me, that's for certain. I knew the man, I acted with him, and I'm going to bury him, but apart from that, there's not a lot I can tell you about him.'

'Did you socialise with him?'

'Mason was not much of a socialiser, neither am I.'

'What do you like to do, Mr Ford?' Tremayne asked.

'I like acting. It gets me away from here. You'd understand if I told you that this job sometimes gets you down.'

'I'd understand,' Tremayne said.

'So would I,' Clare said.

'Apart from acting, what else do you do?'

'I go up to London most weeks. There's always a play on somewhere up there. If I stay here, I only work.'

'Are you married?' Tremayne asked.

'My wife died a few years back.'

'Sorry about that. I was indelicate.'

'Don't worry about it. In our professions, we become only too familiar with the deceased. It's best to maintain a detachment.'

'You never answered my previous question. Is there anyone who may have had a grudge against Mason?'

'I don't think so. We were all united by a love for acting. Apart from that, some socialised with each other, others didn't.'

'Which group did you belong to?'

'A drink of a night after rehearsals, the occasional night out with Freestone and his wife, but apart from that, you'd find me at home.'

'It's not much of a life,' Tremayne said.

'I'm not a gregarious man. The simple pleasures suffice.'

'We're told that Mason did not like Trevor Winston.'

'I can't say that I approve of his behaviour.'

'A religious view?'

'Not at all. It just seems wrong to me. I'd never say that to Winston, though. I get on well enough with him, and I would have thought Winston would have brushed off Mason's occasional jibes.'

'Were there many?'

'Once or twice, but only when Winston messed up his lines.'

'Did he do that often?'

'Not often, but Mason would get annoyed.'

'Would he get annoyed with anyone else if they messed up?'

'No, only with Winston.'

***

Clare, glad to be busy, had found that since the murder at Old Sarum she had slept better. The nights were still restless, but with exhaustion came sleep, and Tremayne, if nothing else, was a determined man.

So far the case had revealed nothing that could indicate a reason for Gordon Mason's murder, no obvious suspect either. The fact that Trevor Winston was gay and Mason did not approve seemed inconsequential.

'What do we know about the murder weapons?' Tremayne asked. It was early in the office, the usual procedure when there was a murder to be solved.

'It would have needed someone with a degree of skill to modify them,' Clare said, not that she had a great deal of knowledge on the subject.

'We've not interviewed all the possible suspects yet.'

'It could still be someone who didn't know that their dagger was more than a toy.'

'According to Hughes, that was unlikely. The pressure of the fake compared to a blade entering a body would have been obvious.'

'To him, it may have been, but Jimmy Francombe said he wouldn't have known.'

'It's a possibility. Does that mean that it could have been someone other than the seven conspirators?'

'It's always possible.'

'If a small metal rod was inserted then that dagger could have become lethal, but how did the person ensure who was going to pick up the correct daggers?' Tremayne asked.

'Does it matter?'

'I think it does.'

'What do you mean?'

'According to Shakespeare, Casca stabs Caesar first, a non-fatal stab in the back, and then Brutus is the final of the assassins.'

'And Brutus only has one stab to the heart.'

'Which means,' Tremayne said, 'that Julius Caesar was not dead when Brutus stabbed him.'

'Does it, guv?'

'Isn't Brutus meant to be separated from Caesar, and Caesar staggers over to his friend after the others have finished and utters the immortal lines? YouTube last night. Marlon Brando as Mark Antony, John Gielgud as Cassius, before you comment.'

'Did Mason stagger over to Peter Freestone at Old Sarum?'

'I'm not sure. I was bored by then,' Tremayne said.

'It may suit your image, guv, but you were enjoying it up there.'

'Don't get ahead of yourself, Yarwood.'

'Anyway, I've no idea,' Clare said. 'I didn't look either.'

'Which means, if he didn't, he could have been dead, held up by the others.'

'You're not accusing all of them of being involved.'

'That's highly unlikely. If Mason's death was the intended result, it's a bit hit and miss.'

'With all that was going on, it was unlikely that the two murderers would have been able to accurately insert their blades in the right places, which means that Mason could have lived.'

'For a while, but he had five wounds.'

'So we can assume that the end result would be death. When he finally collapsed he didn't move again.'

'Which means that someone was certain that he would be dead.'

'Only Freestone had the opportunity to place the blade precisely.'

'It's still speculation, guv.'

'It's good policing, that's what it is.'

'A visit to Freestone?'

'Not yet. Who else have we got to interview?'

'Geoff Pearson, and then Gary Barker and Cheryl Milledge.'

'The town bike.'

'Don't let Superintendent Moulton hear you saying that,' Clare said.

'Why? We're looking for motives here, not Sunday School teachers. If she's got a background, then she's got skeletons.'

'We'll interview Pearson first. He's in Southampton at the university there.'

'Yarwood, you can drive.'

Clare noticed Tremayne pick up his newspaper. 'You'll not get to the races this weekend.'

'That's why you're driving. I need to check the form. I can place my bets online.'

'Bets?'

'Okay, some lose, some win. A man has got to have a hobby. What do you expect me to do, take up stamp collecting?'

'An interesting thought, but you don't look like a stamp collector.'

'I look like your senior, be careful with the lip.'

As they left the office, Clare was glad to be back. She had missed the curmudgeon with his inability to pick a winning horse, his questionable attempts at ironing his shirt with its frayed collar, and his drive to solve a murder.

***

Southampton, the largest city in the area, was only twenty miles away. Clare phoned ahead to ensure that Pearson would be available. Thirty-five minutes after leaving Salisbury, they were seated in the cafeteria at the university.

'I'm studying archaeology and anthropology. It's a three-year course, I'm hopeful of finishing in two.'

'Is there much money in that?' Tremayne asked.

'There's enough. It's a vocation, at least to me. The same as policing, I assume.'

'A lifetime of poverty then.'

'You're probably right,' Pearson said.

'We need to understand what happened,' Clare said. In the daylight, she could see that Pearson was an attractive man in his late twenties. Apart from a scar on his face, she would have described him as handsome. He was also well-dressed.

'Mason could be a tyrant, but I couldn't wish him dead.'

'That's the first time we've heard him called a tyrant,' Tremayne said. He was sipping a cup of tea that Clare had purchased for him. It tasted of cardboard, but Tremayne had thanked her. She was still at the sensitive stage, he could see that, and his acerbic comments were moderated, but her observation about his betting skills had struck a tender spot, the reason he had told her to be careful. Not that he meant it, he knew that, but everyone wanted to offer a comment as to how he was wasting his money, but what did it matter. He didn't throw his money

40

away on trivialities, such as clothing, and he could see that Yarwood spent plenty. Even Geoff Pearson, judging by his clothes and the expensive laptop he had placed on the table, spent more than his fair share, and he was at university, supposedly studying hard with no income.

Betting on the horses, to Tremayne, was his hobby; the fact that he was not very good at it did not change the fact that it kept him occupied when there was no case, a healthy distraction when there was.

'Tyrant may be a little extreme,' Pearson said. 'Did you know the man, when he was alive, that is?'

'I don't remember him. I know Peter Freestone though.'

'It's not surprising you didn't know Gordon Mason. The man was one of life's morose people.'

'What do you mean?' Clare asked.

'A negative personality, the sort of person that after five minutes in their company, you'd end up leaving sadder than when you had first met.'

'Elaborate on that statement,' Tremayne said.

'Okay. The man did not like alcohol, gays, lesbians, anyone not like him.'

'How would you describe him?' Clare asked.

'A killjoy. The type of person you'd not invite to a party.'

'Would he have come?'

'Not to one of mine anyway.'

'Why's that?'

'I'm twenty-six. What sort of parties would you think they are?'

'A lot of alcohol, a lot of sex, a lot of people having a good time,' Tremayne said.

'I'll agree with your first and last analysis, not so sure about the sex,' Pearson replied. He looked over at Clare and smiled.

'Did Mason approve of you?'

'He thought I was brash, a little too sure of myself.'

'Are you?'

'I'm always confident, never let anything get me down. Mason used to get angry in rehearsals. I'd see the positives, he'd be looking for the negatives. I'm a cup half full, he was a cup half empty.'

'His dislike for you, a reason to wish him harm?'

'Not me. I always used to have a laugh at him.'

'To his face?'

'In the pub afterwards with Gary and Cheryl.'

'Gary Barker and Cheryl Milledge?'

'I'm friendly with them.'

'We're told that Gary Barker is not an ambitious person,' Clare said.

'That's true, but I choose my friends based on whether I like them or not. I'm not their judge. If Gary wants to drift that's up to him. Personally, I don't.'

'And Cheryl Milledge?'

'What have you heard?' Pearson asked.

'We're asking the questions,' Tremayne said.

'I've known Cheryl for a few years, a heart of gold. She's a drinker, more than Gary, more than me. She's been around.'

'Been around?' Clare said.

'She had a reputation as being easy when she was younger.'

'Was she?'

'Since she's latched on to Gary, she's changed.'

'For the better?'

'I'd say so. She still drinks too much, and she's got a raucous laugh, but as I've said, a good person. She'd give you the last coin in her pocket if she had to.'

'Does she have money?'

'Enough for a beat-up old car, and a half share of the rent on a bedsit up Devizes Road she shares with Gary.'

'Is that sufficient for her?'

'They don't want much out of life.'

'As compared to you.'

'I want to do archaeology. It's not the way to a fortune unless you can get a programme on television, old ruins of England, that sort of thing.'

'Is that part of your plan?'

'It's in the back of my mind. You need to be pushy, presentable. I think I've got it.'

'You've got plenty of brass, I'll give you that,' Tremayne said. Clare could tell that the DI liked the young man.

'Who would want Gordon Mason dead?' Clare asked.

'I'm not sure. Not many of us liked the man, but he was easy to ignore. Why would anyone want to kill someone else? It makes no sense to me.'

'Gary Barker, Cheryl Milledge?'

'Not a chance. They're harmless, even if a little rough around the edges.'

'Are they?' Tremayne said.

'You know about Cheryl. Gary just goes with the flow. His language can be a bit colourful.'

'Swears a lot?'

'Not when he's sober, but after a few drinks, he will. You've probably seen him around.'

'I don't recollect him.'

'You will, once he's had a few.'

Chapter 6

The last time that Clare had had fish and chips out of a cardboard box was in Bournemouth, not more than a forty-minute drive from Southampton. Then it had been accompanied by a bottle of wine and a wedding proposal from Harry Holchester, but now it was with Tremayne. He had insisted on stopping to eat before they carried on; she would have preferred a sandwich.

She enjoyed being with the man, watching his technique, observing his mannerisms, his foibles. For a man who pretended not to be intellectual, not personable, not caring, he was letting his guard slip, at least with her.

Behind that rough exterior there was a man who cared, an intelligent man who could collate all the evidence they were gathering, all the information about the people they were interviewing, and come up with a reasoned chain of events, a motive, a culprit.

'Come on, Yarwood, the day's young,' Tremayne said. He was out of his chair, his oily chips gone, the fish, if it was indeed fish, gone as well.

Clare took her box with its half-eaten contents and dumped it in the bin at the door. She made a note to not come back to the greasy shop, its disinterested staff behind the counter slapping the fish in batter and then in the boiling oil.

She looked at her watch. It was two in the afternoon.

'We'll find Gary Barker at his work. You've got the number?'

'I'll phone him.'

'Good. You've got the keys,' Tremayne said. It was good that she enjoyed driving, Clare thought. If she was there, she was in the driving seat, while he took the opportunity to catch up on a

little shut-eye, the horses, or just to lie back, close his eyes and
consider the case.

They found Gary Barker working at a garden centre close
to the river in Harnham, a pretty part of the city. Apart from the
weather, which was wet, and the mud underfoot where Barker
was busy with a spade, it would have been pleasant.

'Sorry, I've got to get the plants in the ground today. If I
leave them, they may not take.'

'You know a lot about gardening?' Tremayne asked.

'Green thumb. You're here about Mason?'

'I wouldn't be standing here if it wasn't important.'

'Five minutes, and I'll be with you.'

Ten minutes later, instead of the five, Gary Barker graced
them with his presence. The three were sitting in a greenhouse to
one side of the office. 'They don't like me slacking,' he said.

'We're here investigating a murder. Surely they'll
understand.'

'Not them, a miserable pair.'

'I could square it with them,' Tremayne said.

'They don't hold with acting either, and they positively
hate Cheryl.'

'Why are you concerned with what they think?' Clare
asked.

'They're my parents, not that I let too many people know
that.'

'Why do they hate Cheryl?'

'My parents, old school.'

'What do you mean?'

'Seeing the young lady's here, I'm not sure I want to say.'

'I'm a police officer,' Clare said. 'Say what you need to.'

'I'm the only son, and those two, my parents, have some
dated ideas.'

'I'm not sure we understand.'

'Back when they were married, it was one man, one
woman, virgin on the wedding night, total fidelity, a glass of wine
at Christmas.'

'They must have liked Gordon Mason.'

'He was their sort of man.'

'Was he yours?'

'What do you think? It wasn't as if I hated him. I just ignored him, laughed it off, had a few jokes in the pub at his expense.'

'Your parents part of the joke as well?'

'I don't tell anyone about them unless it's important.'

'It's important now.'

'That's why I'm telling you. Anyway, back to Cheryl. I love the woman.'

'We're aware that she has a chequered past,' Clare said.

'Chequered, that's a good word. Cheryl, God bless her, has had a chequered past: married once, engaged to another, lived with a couple of other men.'

'And your parents disapprove?'

'To them, she's the devil's spawn.'

'To you?' Clare asked.

'We're kindred spirits. I've got a few things that I regret. I deal with the present and Cheryl's with me. What she may have done in the past is none of my concern, and it's certainly not my parents' either.'

'Have they met her?'

'Once. They didn't like her. It ended badly.'

'Are you the only son?'

'That's what they don't like. My father's not well, another few months, no more, and my mother's starting to forget.'

'You'll inherit?'

'Yes. Don't tell anyone if you don't have to. Everyone sees me as a loser, but I'm not. I could make something of this place.'

'And they don't want Cheryl involved?' Clare said.

'They don't want anyone involved, not even me, but with Cheryl, it's venomous.'

'You played Cinna?' Tremayne asked.

'That's where we met, at the dramatic society, Cheryl and me.'

'You're both keen?'

'We love dressing up, and we take it very seriously.'

'Did you have any problems with Gordon Mason?'

'Not me. He'd sometimes go on to Cheryl about her being a fallen woman.'

'How did you take it? How did she?'

'She'd give him the sharp edge of her tongue.'

'And you?'

'He'd not talk to me unless it was necessary.'

'Because of your parents?'

'He got on well enough with them. I know they've tried to stitch me up, negate my inheritance. They took advice from Mason.'

'Were they successful?'

'I keep my eyes peeled. I saw the correspondence.'

'What did you do?'

'I took legal advice.'

'Does Cheryl know about this?'

'Not in detail. She'd be the classic bull in the China shop.'

'And you need a subtle approach?' Clare said.

'They could always run down the garden centre, sell it for a pittance.'

'Would they do that?'

'They're total bastards, so was Mason. The three of them, Bible-bashing hypocrites.'

'It's a motive to kill Mason.'

'That's why I've told you. If you'd found it out from someone else, it would reflect badly on Cheryl and me. I only need to wait a few more months, and this place is mine. We've got great plans for here. Cheryl's a smart woman, she'll look after the administration and the financial; I'll look after the plants.'

'We need to talk to Cheryl,' Clare said.

'Seven this evening, 156 Devizes Road. Is that fine by you?'

'That's fine,' Tremayne said.

***

It was late afternoon before the two police officers left Gary Barker, not long enough to interview anyone else before meeting Barker's girlfriend. Instead, they returned to the police station on Bemerton Road. Superintendent Moulton was in the reception area as they entered. 'Good to see you back, Sergeant Yarwood,' he said.

'Thank you, sir,' Clare replied.

'How's the case going, DI?' Moulton asked.

'We're interviewing the suspects. There are a few that have motives.'

'An arrest soon?'

'We're working on it.'

'Keep up the good work,' Moulton said as he left the building.

'A changed man,' Clare said.

'Another few weeks and he'll be on about my retirement again,' Tremayne said.

'You don't like him much, do you?'

'What gave you that idea?'

'Your curtness with him.'

'Why pretend? He doesn't think much of me, I don't think much of him. You'll learn, Yarwood. You don't need to be friendly to everyone. Do your job, take no nonsense, get results; they're more important.'

'Office politics?'

'If you're Moulton, but you're not. You're shaping up to be a good officer.'

'Shaping up?'

'You're not there yet. Stick with me, and you will be.'

'That's what I intend to do. What do you reckon to those we've interviewed so far?'

The two had settled themselves back in Tremayne's office. The man was leaning back on his chair again, the front two legs off the ground.

'Barker had a reason to dislike the man; I'd say it was sufficient as a motive.'

'Could Barker's solicitor put on a caveat to prevent a sale?' Clare said.

'That seems weak to me. Check it out, see what you can find. If his parents own the business, then how can its sale be stopped? I know there are laws about divesting assets to the children to save on inheritance tax, but that doesn't apply here. It's strange that Gary Barker was so affable, yet, according to him, his parents are total bastards.'

'Maybe they aren't. We need to talk to them.'

'Not today. We've got an appointment.'

'Do you want me to drive?' Clare asked.

'What do you think?'

***

For someone who was hopeful of taking over his parent's garden centre and the house that came with it, Gary Barker and Cheryl Milledge's bedsit did not impress either of the two police officers. The first-floor apartment with a fold-down bed secured to the wall was not a place that Clare warmed to, nor did Tremayne. Clare knew his style of living, having been to his house on a couple of occasions. It was nothing special, he'd admit to that, singularly lacking in any of the touches that convert a house into a home. Cheryl Milledge was a busty individual; Clare could not describe her as beautiful, or even attractive. However, the woman was welcoming on their arrival.

'Take a seat,' she said. Clare looked around in dismay. Every possible space was covered with magazines or old newspapers. 'Here, that'll do,' Cheryl said, as she pushed a pile of papers to one side.

'Sorry about the mess,' Barker said. 'We're normally tidier.' Clare doubted the man.

'You're here about Gordon Mason,' Cheryl said. 'Do you fancy a beer?'

Tremayne certainly did; it had been a long day. 'No, thanks,' he said. Beer and policing did not mix. He'd buy one later at the pub. For now, they had to find out from Cheryl Milledge what she knew.

'You played Brutus's wife?' Clare said.

'Portia.'

'A good part?'

'I'd have preferred Calpurnia, but I'm not married to one of Salisbury's leading estate agents.'

'Is that important?'

'It is with the Salisbury Amateur Dramatic Society.'

'What does Fiona Dowling have that you don't?'

'It's not acting ability. She couldn't act her way out of a paper bag, although she's managed to convince her husband that she's faithful.'

'You shouldn't say that,' Barker said.

'They're the police. They'll find out later, and we'll be suspect if we hold back. That's how it works, isn't it, Detective Inspector?'

'The truth is always best. We will corroborate any information received, careful not to reveal our source.'

'It may be best if you tell us the full story,' Clare said.

'Hang on while I get another beer. Are you sure you don't want one?' Cheryl said.

One minute later she returned, handing her boyfriend a can as well. 'You've met Geoff Pearson?'

'Today, in Southampton.'

'He's a friend of ours, or at least we drink together.'

'What about him?'

'He's screwing Fiona Dowling.'

'He's younger than her,' Clare said.

'Has Pearson told you this?'

'Not him, he's smart. We've teased him a few times after a few beers, but he'll not talk.'

'Then where's your proof?'

'I caught them at it hammer and tongs once.'

'Where?'

'We sometimes meet at the Dowlings' house to rehearse. One time, Len's not there. No idea where he is, but we carried on anyway. Fiona, she put on a spread of food, drinks. I drank more than I should, but I do that all too often. I'm trying to cut back, but you know?'

Clare didn't know, but she did not intend to comment.

'Mason's there casting accusing looks at me, but he's got no right to complain.'

'What does that mean?' Tremayne asked.

'I'll come back to it.'

'Cheryl, it's not right to tell them,' Barker said.

'Wise up, Gary. They're police officers, they'll find this out eventually. I'm just helping them.'

'Carry on, please,' Clare said.

'We've all left, or I thought we all had. I'm outside the house, desperate to go to the toilet. I would have gone on the flowers, but Mason's still hanging around, as is Bill Ford.'

'Peter Freestone, Jimmy Francombe, Phillip Dennison?'

'I don't know about them. If they had been there, I'd have still gone on the flowers. Mason freaked me out. Anyway, I'm there bursting, the front door's still open. I go in and dash for the toilet. There's one downstairs. I forget to pull the flush. As I'm coming out, still pulling up my jeans, I can hear a sound in the other room. I'm feeling better by this time. There are two people, their voices are low.'

'Who was it?'

'I'm coming to that. I'm careful, and I take off my shoes and creep along the hallway. The door to the dining room is open. There on the floor, Fiona, flat on her back, Geoff Pearson on top of her going for his life.'

'Sexual intercourse?' Clare asked.

'What do you think they were doing, playing monopoly? It was full on, let me tell you.'

'Did they see you?'

'Geoff did.'

'What did he do?'

'He pushed the door shut with one of his feet.'

'Did Fiona Dowling see you?'

'Not a chance. She was in second heaven by then.'

'Afterwards, did he confirm it?'

'He'd only smile if I asked.'

'Are they still involved?'

'We've both seen her looking over at him at rehearsals. They're still into it. Apparently, Len Dowling, the full of himself, hotshot estate agent, is a lousy lover.'

'How do you know that?' Clare asked.

'That's what I've been told,' Cheryl Milledge said. Clare knew where that information had come from, from Cheryl Milledge herself. Clare could see why she had such a dreadful reputation.

'You mentioned Gordon Mason before,' Tremayne reminded the woman.

'We put on a play at a church hall. I forget the production, but there's a kissing scene with Mason and me.'

'You agreed?'

'We're acting. I didn't need to like the man.'

'How about him? Was he comfortable with it?'

'He seemed to be. In rehearsals, we just pretended, held each other, made the motions, no contact.'

'I assume that was not the case when you presented it to the public,' Clare said.

'There's an audience, about eighty people, some children. It's time for our scene. We're there professing our love for each other, sealing it with a kiss. It's a darkened room on the stage. I come over to him, act the part, put my arms around his shoulders, he puts his arms around my waist. That's when it went astray.'

'Overly amorous?' Clare said.

'The man pulls me in close. I can feel the erection, and then he rams his tongue down my throat.'

"What did you do?"

'What could I do? I acted out the scene, quicker than I should have, and pulled away. The audience never realised what was going on.'

'And afterwards?'

52

'I put my fist into his face once we were backstage. Nothing more was said after that.'

'You could have reported him.'

'What's the point? No one will listen to me, and it wasn't the first time a man has thrust his unwanted affections on to me. And besides, I wanted to continue to act.'

Chapter 7

Phillip Dennison adopted a haughty tone when Tremayne and Clare arrived at his house. It was clear the man was loaded. In the driveway, an Aston Martin.

'Beautiful car,' Tremayne said, in an attempt to break the ice.

'Paid cash for it,' Dennison said. Tremayne sighed, realising that the man liked to flaunt his wealth.

Tremayne had no interest in the Aston Martin, although Clare liked it. Once inside the house, more a mansion, they were ushered into the main room. The walls were lined with oil paintings, a grand piano stood in one corner, its lid raised.

'I like to play it every day,' Dennison said. For a man in his fifties, he had a healthy tan, not the result of an English climate. He was dressed in a pair of beige-coloured trousers and a polo shirt, the type that Harry had liked.

'Gordon Mason?' Tremayne said.

'Tragic, tragic,' Dennison said. Clare could hear the insincerity in his voice.

'You were playing Mark Antony?'

'That's correct.'

'If you don't mind me being blunt,' Tremayne said out of courtesy, not out of concern for the man.

'Not at all.'

'Why were you involved with the local dramatic society? You're obviously wealthy, well connected. Surely you must have better opportunities elsewhere.'

'If you mean, could I afford to sign on for acting classes in London, use my contacts to attend workshops with some of the best actors, then, yes, I could.'

'Why don't you?'

'The Salisbury Amateur Dramatic Society is a diversion from the normal stresses. I go there, enjoy myself, mingle with them, rich and poor. I enjoy it greatly.'

'What do you do for a living?'

'I play the financial markets, very successful actually. Each day, I'll trade on the price of one commodity going up or down against another. Some days, I'll make a small fortune, other days I'll lose it. It's high stress, high reward, high risk. I could ease the stress with alcohol, with a mistress, or with golf. Acting is my outlet, and if it's a local production where I get to stand up on stage and say a few lines, then that's fine by me.'

'I understand,' Clare said.

'I'm sorry about your loss. I truly am.'

'You knew Harry?'

'We went to school together. We stayed in touch on an occasional basis.'

'I'll be fine. Thank you for your concern.'

A woman came breezing into the room; Clare was taken aback by the look of her.

'I'm Samantha,' she said, as she made a beeline for Tremayne, warmly shaking his hand.

You're wasting your time there, the man's got no money, Clare thought.

'Pleased to meet you,' Tremayne replied, sucking in his stomach at the same time.

The woman dressed expensively, her hair was blonde and out of a bottle, her jewellery designed to order from what Clare could tell. She was the sort of woman that men lusted after, and she knew it. 'What's Phillip been up to? Cheating the old ladies out of their savings?' she asked.

'We're investigating the death of Gordon Mason.'

'Oh, him.'

'Did you know him?'

'Phillip dragged me along one night to one of their productions. For the life of me, I can't see why he bothers.'

'It's an outlet for me, you know that.'

Clare could see, she assumed that Tremayne did as well, that the trophy wife and her older husband did not get on. The arrangement was financial, in that he had the money and she wanted it. Apart from that, there was the appearance of love, the reality of disdain.

'Gordon Mason was murdered.'

'Phillip mentioned it.'

'Did it concern you?'

'Why? Should it?'

'The man was a fellow actor of your husband.'

'Acting, is that what you call it? A bunch of locals pretending that they have talent, and as for Mason, the man was a pig.'

Clare could understand her contempt for Mason, in that if he had not liked Winston with his effeminate manner or Cheryl Milledge with her promiscuous past, he was probably not going to like the woman standing in front of them, even if she was exquisite. Clare had to admit she was an attractive woman until she opened her mouth. From there on, it was constant abuse against her husband. She didn't understand why he put up with it, or she with him, but then Clare knew that her family had money, as did Harry, and what she had wanted was love, nothing more. Her parents were cold, Harry was not.

'My wife's not a fan of my nights out. I've asked her to accompany me, but she'll not come.'

'You're right there. I've got better things to do.'

'If you'd excuse us, Mrs Dennison,' Tremayne said, 'we need to talk to your husband alone.'

'I'm off anyway. I'm going to hit the shops again.'

The woman left, jumped into the driver's seat of the Aston Martin and accelerated out of the driveway.

'She's not normally like that,' Dennison said.

'That's fine,' Tremayne said, knowing full well that she was. His wife had been a person who had loved him, showed encouragement, even tolerated his funny ways. He still missed her after all these years of being on his own. He could see that Dennison, for all his wealth, his younger wife, no doubt very physical in keeping the man young in her bed, was not a contented person.

'Did you like Gordon Mason?' Clare asked.

'Honestly, not very much. It doesn't qualify as a motive.'

'We're not accusing you or anyone else at this time. We're just interviewing everyone who was up at Old Sarum. Can we come back to the previous question? Did you like Gordon Mason?'

'I despised him.'

'Yet you acted with him.'

'It was my outlet.'

'From the stresses here?' Clare said.

'It's not only work-related.'

'Your wife? My apologies if it seems as if I'm prying, but we need to know all the facts, no matter how irrelevant they may seem.'

'I'm not sure if my wife is relevant, but yes, there are difficulties.'

'Are you able to elaborate?' Tremayne said.

'I've told you. Some days I'm flush with money, others I'm not. My wife does not moderate her behaviour.'

'She continues to spend,' Clare said.

'Don't judge her for what she is. I knew that when we married, and she knew that I saw her as a reward.'

'Was she?' Tremayne asked.

'At first. Holidays overseas, expensive nights out, but now it doesn't have the same interest. If it weren't for my wife, I'd cash in, take a small place in Salisbury and enjoy myself. It's the ageing process unfortunately. I want a quieter life, she does not.'

'And the dramatic society is part of that quieter life?'

'I know it's only a group of locals having fun, but we enjoy ourselves, and believe me, we put on a good play.'

'We were told that you have a superior bearing, as if you see yourself as better than them.'

'It's not that. I arrive in an Aston Martin, I speak with a refined accent, but I don't aim to put anyone down.'

'Cheryl Milledge for example.'

'Earthy woman, I like her. She's not out to bleed some silly old fool out of his money. She's there with Gary, not the smartest guy, but they seem happy. You've heard the saying "if I only had money". Well, I do, and it's not all it's cracked up to be.'

'Coming back to the night of Gordon Mason's death,' Tremayne said.

'I wasn't involved in the assassination. I wasn't even there.'

'You weren't on the stage.'

'I was around the back, waiting for my cue.'

'Where was Caesar's body when Brutus was addressing the crowd?'

'To one side of the stage.'

'In the play, it is Mark Antony that comes out from the Senate with Caesar's body.'

'That's true. There's a period when the conspirators are outside with Brutus, attempting to justify their actions to the crowd.'

'And you're alone with Caesar's body.'

'In the play, but up at Old Sarum, he's off to one side, lying down with his tunic over his body and face.'

'Did you speak to him when he was lying there?'

'No.'

'Any reason?'

'I act with the man. I don't talk to him.'

'That much animosity?'

'I've told you. I did not like the man.'

'Did he criticise you because of your wife?'

'He called her a tart, selling herself to an old man.'

'How did you take that?'

'What do you think?'

'When was this?'

'The only time I took her to one of our productions. Six months ago.'

'And you still continued to act with him?'

'It was my outlet, and besides, he wasn't far off the mark.'

'That's a damning comment about your wife,' Tremayne said.

'Is it? You're here investigating a murder. There's no point in trying to pretend. My wife is here because I'm rich. I married her because she's young and she made me feel young. There's no pretence on either side of the marriage.'

'Did you kill Mason?' Tremayne asked.

'How? I wasn't one of the assassins.'

***

Of all the key players that night in Old Sarum, only one remained to be interviewed, the notorious Fiona Dowling, if Chery Milledge's statement about the woman and Geoff Pearson was correct. They found her at home.

'I played Calpurnia,' Fiona Dowling said. She was smartly dressed, in her mid to late thirties, and, as could be seen, a woman comfortable with herself.

'We know that Gordon Mason was stabbed thirty-four times.'

'Thirty-three in the play. Act 5, Scene 1: *Never, until Caesar's thirty-three wounds are well avenged, or until I too have been killed by you,*' Fiona Dowling said.

'That's the play. Mason was stabbed thirty-four times at Old Sarum; five of those stabs entered his body.'

'Poor Gordon,' Fiona Dowling said.

'You've expressed concern for the man,' Clare said.

'It's a figure of speech.'

'Did you like him?'

'He was a strange character, almost out of time.'

'What do you mean?'

'His prudish views, his intolerance.'

'Were you like him?'

'Not in my views, but I represented the values he admired.'

'What values were those?' Clare asked.

'Loyal wife, faithful to my husband, good mother.'

Clare wasn't sure what to say next. If it weren't a police investigation, she would have commented on the accusation that she was having an affair with Geoff Pearson, but that wasn't proven yet. If it was, then Cheryl Milledge with her past, Samantha Dennison with her older husband were better people, in that they were honest about what they were.

Fiona Dowling may have looked saintly, but if she was involved with Pearson, her husband oblivious to the fact, then there was intrigue, possible motives for murder.

'Let us go back to that night at Old Sarum,' Tremayne said. The three of them were sitting in the dining room, the room where Fiona Dowling and Geoff Pearson had writhed in passion on the floor. Tremayne could see Clare looking for the spot, nodding his head for her to focus on the woman.

'I was waiting backstage for my cue.'

'Did you see anything suspicious?'

'No. It was fairly dark back there, as you know. We have a backdrop on the stage, and our changing rooms were there and behind some ruins. Apart from that, I just sat and waited.'

'Cheryl Milledge would have liked to play Calpurnia.'

'Cheryl's always pushing for the lead female role.'

'Is there any reason why you were given the role of Caesar's wife?'

'Has Cheryl said anything?'

'Not at all. We're trying to find out the relationships between the actors and Gordon Mason, that's all.'

'Cheryl may tell you different, but I'm a better actor than her. The fact that Len sponsors our productions is not important. Peter Freestone would not allow the production to be affected due to nepotism.'

'Ancient Rome was full of nepotism,' Clare said.

'Maybe it was, but we aren't.'

'Tell us about the other actors and your relationship with them.'

'Is this relevant? I've got to pick up the children from school. I wasn't on the stage, I didn't thrust a dagger into Gordon. What else is there?'

'You were backstage with the daggers.'

'So were Cheryl and Phillip Dennison.'

60

'Did they touch the daggers at any time?'

'Not that I saw. They were in a box, anyone could have touched them. We used the daggers in rehearsals. They were fakes, okay for spreading butter, not for killing someone.'

'Were they?'

'At rehearsals they were. I ran my finger along the blade of one.'

'Blunt?'

'It would open a letter, I suppose, but nothing more.'

'And how long ago was that?'

'Our last full-dress rehearsal. Two days before Old Sarum.'

'The other actors?' Tremayne said.

'Peter Freestone likes to take charge. Cheryl Milledge, competent, keen, well known around Salisbury.'

'Well known?' Clare said.

'We were in the same class at school. We were both a bit free with it back then, but I settled down, Cheryl discovered alcohol.'

'Free?' Clare said.

'Men, really boys back then. I met Len, decided he was the man for me. Cheryl continued playing the field, still is, or at least she was until she met Gary.'

'Faithful to him?'

'I've no idea. She's got no money, neither has Gary, although that never meant much to her.'

'And it did to you?'

'When I met Len, he had nothing, the son of a postman. We made the business together.'

'The others?' Tremayne said.

'Trevor Winston, good hairdresser. I go there myself. He's gay, but that doesn't concern me. Bill Ford, decent. Jimmy Francombe, full of hormones, always eyeing Cheryl and me.'

'Visually undressing you,' Clare said.

'He's given you the treatment?'

'Yes.'

'Phillip Dennison?'

'Bitch of a wife.'

'You've met her?'

'He brought her along once. She bothered Gordon, but I took no notice. I've seen her type before, a tart trying to sell herself off as something better. Take off the war paint and she'd be nothing special.'

'Does her husband know this?'

'He should after Gordon insulted her. I thought the two men were going to come to blows. If Phillip loses his money, she'll be off soon enough.'

'Gary Barker?'

'He's keen on Cheryl. She seems keen on him. They're a matched pair. Whether it will last is anyone's guess.'

'Cheryl's had a few relationships,' Clare said.

'A few, that's as good a way of saying it.'

'Many?' Tremayne said.

'We go back a long way, Cheryl and me.'

'Geoff Pearson?'

Clare looked for a reaction, couldn't see any.

'Smart man, he'll go far. He's charismatic, good with the ladies. No doubt he's got plenty of girlfriends, although he's never brought any along.'

'Your husband?'

'Len, you know. Brash, ambitious, hard-working, good provider. What else is there to say about him.'

'He's full on,' Tremayne said.

'I know he can rub people up the wrong way, but we're close.'

Chapter 8

It was dark by the time Tremayne and Clare arrived back at Bemerton Road Police Station. The two of them had eaten at a Chinese restaurant in Fisherton Street on the way there. For the first time, Clare realised, she had not thought of Harry all day. The preoccupation with the murder enquiry was doing her good.

Back in the office, the two of them drank cups of tea, Clare having made them, regardless of Tremayne's earlier comment that he had only missed her tea making when she had been away for several months.

'What do you think, guv?' Clare asked.

'There's plenty of motives, but are any strong enough to stand up?'

'Not really. There's plenty of petty politics, a few that don't like the others, but it's hardly enough for murder.'

'Don't believe it, Yarwood. People kill for less.'

'Fiona Dowling?'

'Strange, she's the one I trust the least, especially if Cheryl Milledge's story is correct.'

'Any way to prove it?'

'Jim Hughes could check the rug on the floor.'

'Get real, guv. If those two were on it, there's hardly likely to be any proof now.'

'We've focussed on seven assassins, two murderers.'

'They were the only ones who stabbed the man.'

'Were they? Mason's lying on the floor. Is it possible someone else came up and stabbed him again, dealt the fatal blow.'

'It doesn't make sense. Why would the man be lying there if he wasn't dead already?'

'Then why didn't anyone investigate? It couldn't have been comfortable with his face covered.'

'Maybe they did, saw he was dead and left him.'

'If he wasn't dead, then who else could have stabbed him?'

'Mark Antony.'

'Phillip Dennison?'

'He had the motive to want the man dead.'

'The daggers all had blood on them, and Mason had been stabbed with a sharp blade on the stage. If it's Dennison, then his was not the first fatal blow. That would have had to have been one of the assassin's blades.'

'It's plausible, I suppose, but you'll need a better motive than Mason insulted Dennison's wife.'

'The lovely Samantha.'

'Did you think that?' Clare said.

'What do you think, Yarwood?'

'You'd prefer Cheryl Milledge.'

'At least she'll drink a pint of beer with me.'

'If you're paying, you'll need to improve your win rate on the horses.'

'Insults aside, Cheryl Milledge, apart from her atrocious housekeeping, was the only one who opened up with us.'

'I think Samantha Dennison did.'

'How?'

'The way she treated her husband. She knows she's controlling him, and she's taking advantage. She didn't pretend to be anything other than what she is.'

'A gold digger?'

'Mason was more direct, but that's what she is.'

'What's her history? We should check her out.'

'Is she relevant?'

'It's possible. Did Mason have any money? Was he insulting her as a diversion?'

'You're stretching it there.'

'We're clutching at straws, and you know it. We know there are two daggers, five wounds. Do we know which dagger entered where and how many times?'

'We've not asked.'

'It's important. We need to know whether he died on that stage, and if there were any wounds inflicted afterwards.'

***

The dramatic society's performance for the following night at Old Sarum had been cancelled. Peter Freestone had called all the main suspects to his office to discuss what had happened, and what their future held.

'I'd like to express my sorrow at the death of a fellow thespian,' Freestone said.

'We should dedicate our next production to him,' Bill Ford said.

Cheryl Milledge said little. It was eight o'clock in the evening, and she and Gary had had their fair share of alcohol by that time.

'You're a drunk, Cheryl,' Fiona Dowling said. The extraordinary meeting was not going well, Freestone could see that plainly enough.

'Fiona, Cheryl, all of us,' Freestone said, 'the situation is more serious than you believe. We've all been visited by Detective Inspector Tremayne and Detective Sergeant Yarwood. We're all aware of their investigation into how Gordon was killed, and by whom.'

'They're saying that two of us are murderers,' Jimmy Francombe said.

'They have scientific proof to make that statement.'

'Well, I didn't kill him.'

'Jimmy, if you could suppress your boyish enthusiasm for a minute, we need to discuss what we know, and how to proceed.'

Francombe sat still, fuming and glaring over at Freestone.

'Freestone's right,' Bill Ford said. 'If one or two of us are murderers, and I can't believe that, how do we continue?'

'A murder mystery night, is that what you are suggesting?' Phillip Dennison said.

'I'm good at those,' Gary Barker said, temporarily reviving from his alcohol-fuelled stupor.

'I don't think so,' Freestone said. 'The police will do the investigating. We just need to coordinate our approach to them, if that's possible.'

'How? They have forensic and pathology evidence. We'll not be able to outthink them and why should we? Fiona and I have done nothing wrong,' Len Dowling said.

The two Dowlings were sitting close to each other, Geoff Pearson was on the other side of the room. Cheryl Milledge looked across between the three of them, looking for the tell-tale signs of recognition; she couldn't see any, but then she knew the woman from their schooldays, knew her to have been the more promiscuous back then.

'The police said that two of the daggers entered Gordon's body,' Freestone said. 'I only stabbed him the one time, and my knife retracted.'

'How do you know? You had the clearest target,' Len Dowling said. 'And it wasn't me.'

'I'll vouch for my husband,' Fiona Dowling said.

'How can you do that, Fiona?' Gary Barker said.

'I know my husband better than you.'

'And how well does your husband know you?' Cheryl said.

The atmosphere was electric. Everyone knew that within that office were two men who had committed murder. Freestone realised that convening the meeting had been a mistake.

'Maybe none of us killed him,' Pearson said. Fiona looked at him, so did Cheryl.

'How?' Ford said. For once he was not dressed in black, but casual in a pair of jeans and an open-necked shirt.

'Could anyone else have stabbed him before or after?'

'I thought you were smart,' Freestone said. 'That sounds crazy. The man collapses on the ground. Mark Antony comes in, and he's placed on the stretcher. He was dead then.'

'Was he? What if he was only unconscious? Those daggers can hurt, even the fake ones.'

'What are you trying to do? Make out that it was an innocent mistake.'

'Hold on, Freestone. You're getting carried away here,' Dennison said. 'Don't forget that a man died.'

'You despised the man, the same as Trevor did, don't deny it.'

'I didn't despise him,' Trevor Winston said. 'I've had a lifetime of abuse. One bitter old man wasn't going to affect me. I just used to laugh it off.'

'Rubbish, the man used to utter derisory comments in your direction,' Fiona said. 'I used to see the expression on your face.'

'I'm not saying that I liked it, but I had no intention of killing him. If I'd killed everyone who's baited me, beaten me up for what I am, then there'd be a lot of dead bodies, and besides, killing the man because he's a bigot doesn't make sense. Look at Len, look at Mason. One's an estate agent, the other's a solicitor, and you, Peter Freestone, are a councillor here in Salisbury. A dodgy deal, cheating someone out of their property, would make more sense, and then there's Phillip with an expensive lifestyle, an expensive wife. If there was a financial gain, Phillip, would you consider killing him?'

'You little bastard,' Dennison said as he lurched towards Winston.

'Hold back,' Bill Ford said as he grabbed hold of Dennison, Barker grabbing hold of Winston.

'I'm with Freestone,' Ford said. 'We need to be united. Our animosities and prejudices will not help here. Whatever the outcome, two of us wanted the man dead, maybe more, but two that we know of.'

'My apologies to Dennison,' Trevor Winston said'

'Accepted. I understand the tension here,' Dennison replied, although he did not look as if he meant it.

'Ladies, gentlemen, this is getting us nowhere,' Freestone said, attempting to bring the group to order.

'Will you let me speak?' Fiona Dowling said.

'Carry on,' Freestone replied. The man was exasperated, and he had taken his seat, leaning back in dismay. 'I tried,' he said.

'You were right to bring us here tonight,' Fiona said. 'Our lives are in turmoil because of what has happened. Let us not pretend that we liked the man. He had his faults, the same as all of us, so let's not dwell on his unless it's relevant. The police will not give in until they've found whoever was responsible. It's clearly not an accident, in that the daggers had been tampered with.'

'What are you trying to achieve?' Cheryl asked.

'In this room are two people who are capable of violence. We are a disparate group, and whereas some of us will distort the truth if it is to our benefit, the majority of us would not consider murder.'

'What are you getting at?' Len, Fiona's husband, asked.

'Gordon was a good solicitor. He understood the law better than anyone else in this room.'

'Are you suggesting he may have been crooked?' Dennison said.

'What are the options? One, he has dirt on somebody, or two, they have the dirt on him.'

'There are two people.'

'Agreed, but let us consider the possibilities first. Gordon was blackmailing, or he was being blackmailed. That's two options.'

'And the others?'

'He knew something that other people did not want to be revealed. Or he was about to do something that would have been injurious to others.'

'Such as?'

'I don't know. I'm only putting forward theories. Two people in this room know the answer, but which two? Is anyone willing to stand up and tell us why they're innocent?'

'Don't look at me. I'm still at school,' Jimmy Francombe said.

'Any inappropriate gestures from Gordon?' Dennison asked.

'If he had tried anything, I'd have hit him.'

'I did once,' Cheryl said.

'Do you want to elaborate?' Fiona asked. She knew the story. She just wanted her former school friend to feel the heat.

'Last year when we put on that modern play, the one we'd all rather forget.'

'The one where two of us forgot our lines, and the backdrop fell down.'

'Don't mention the name.'

'I won't. Is that when you hit him?' Fiona asked. She was enjoying Cheryl's squirming. After the heated exchanges of five minutes before, she was feeling relaxed again. She had seen Cheryl looking at her, looking at Geoff. Fiona was sure she couldn't know, as they'd always been careful, and Len had no idea. Poor Len, the man of action, barely able to perform in bed, yet always attempting to soothe the men, charm their wives, into parting with their hard-earned cash for an overpriced renovator's delight, most times succeeding.

'The kissing scene, where we had a passionate embrace.'

Everyone in the room was quiet, even Jimmy Francombe, hoping for some titillation, something to tell his friends.

'What happened?' Fiona egged Cheryl on.

'We're meant to lock lips, but he's there forcing his tongue down my throat, pushing his groin into me.'

'What did you do?' Freestone asked.

'I would have kneed him in the groin if it wasn't on stage. Instead, I hurried the scene. Later backstage, I confronted him.'

'What did he say?'

'There wasn't much he could say with my fist in his mouth.'

'Why didn't you tell us?'

'He's not the first man that's tried it on. I dealt with him in the only language that he understood.'

'Did he try it again?'

'Not him. Others have fancied their chances.'

'Who?' Fiona asked.

'It's not important unless they want to be bent over grabbing their balls the next time.'

'I had no issue with the man,' Pearson said. 'He was polite with me, acted his part. We were always civil, but we had nothing in common.'

'Apart from a love of ancient monuments,' Dennison said.

'Are you referring to that monstrosity of a house that he lived in?'

'What style is it?'

'I agree it's a grim looking place, overgrown, almost Gothic, but it's only seventy years old. My interest goes back further than that. Medieval and earlier is what I'm interested in.'

'You could still have killed him.'

'What for? I'm at university, my life before me. I don't want to spend time in prison for the murder of a bigot.'

'Is that how you see him?' Fiona said.

'What do you want us to say? Do you want us to defend him? Who liked him? Is there anyone willing to put up their hand and say that?'

'You've made your point,' Freestone said. The atmosphere in the room was improved. Dennison looked as if he was ready to leave, Gary and Cheryl looked as though they needed another drink, and Fiona was looking at Pearson. Len Dowling was surveying the room, focussing on his wife and Pearson. He said nothing.

'I suggest that we cancel next week's meeting,' Freestone said.

'I'll second that. We'll not be able to work together until whoever killed Mason is arrested. Whatever happens, we'll be short of a couple of actors,' Ford said.

Nobody said anything, apart from a shaking of the heads, a denial of involvement.

Chapter 9

Clare never enjoyed the visits to Pathology, and there she was, twice in the one week.

'Tremayne, I thought I'd seen the last of you,' Collins, the pathologist, said.

'I couldn't keep away. We need five minutes of your time,' Tremayne said.

'Which means ten. Carry on, what do you want to know?'

'Is it possible that Gordon Mason did not die on the stage?'

'It's possible, but he had been knifed five times, two of the wounds were fatal.'

'I'll accept that, but is it possible that one or two of the wounds could have been inflicted at the time the body was not visible.'

'After the assassination and when Mark Antony comes out from the Senate with the body?'

'That's it.'

'It's possible, I suppose. It's not a situation I've considered.'

'But it's still possible.'

'I'd be willing to consider it, although I have difficulty with all of the wounds being inflicted off the stage.'

'That's not what concerns me.'

'What then?'

'We've seven assassins, as well as Mark Antony. I just want to know if Mark Antony, or at least the actor, could have stabbed Mason as well.'

'Anyone could have if it was out of sight.'

'Even a woman?'

'Why not? Do you have any suspects?'

'There are others that I would consider.'

'What about the stretcher bearers, the crowd outside, the servants?'

'They changed their clothes, depending on their part. We're working with the ten, possibly eleven.'

'It's not possible to give you an exact time of death, other than within a one-hour period. That will allow the stabbing to have occurred on the stage, or behind the scenes. Whatever happened, he would have been dead when he was brought out for Mark Antony's denouncement of Brutus.'

'Any reason?'

'Yet again, it seems illogical. The man was stabbed on the stage; he's in agony and dying, and you expect him to remain motionless for another thirty to sixty minutes. It just doesn't make sense, that's all. I'll still hold to my opinion that he died on that stage and that neither Mark Antony nor Calpurnia and Portia were involved.'

'I'll still keep my options open. One more thing, you've been able to ascertain that two different blades were used.'

'Yes.'

'How?'

'Imperfections in the blades.'

'The two blades in the heart, were they different or the one dagger?'

'Two. I believe I've told you this before.'

'I just needed to double-check.'

'Mark Antony, sorry, Phillip Dennison, could be one of those involved or totally innocent,' Clare said.

'We need to check him further. Maybe we can dismiss some of the others, the young man for instance.'

'Why?'

'Where's the motive?' Tremayne said.

'I can't see it at this point in time, but murdering someone just because they called you young or gay or drunk hardly seems to be a reason.'

'It may do to the person being called it. We don't know the mental state of these people. They're an unusual bunch, that's for sure.'

'You're getting the hang of it now, Yarwood.'

'Are you putting me on the spot, testing me out?'

'Not totally. I'm throwing up ideas, seeing where they fall. We can't cover everyone with the same intensity, we need to prioritise, and we need a damn good motive.'

'We'll not find it here in Dr Collins' office,' Clare said.

'Thank you, Sergeant. Please take Tremayne out of here and let me get on with my work.'

***

Tremayne, a perceptive man, able to separate the circumstantial from the relevant, had to admit confusion as to who the murderer was. There were plenty of reasons to dislike Gordon Mason, none sufficient to kill him. 'Yarwood, what's your take on this?' he asked.

'Why kill the man? He's the sort of person that you meet from time to time but learn to ignore. If all the negatives against him are correct, it only shows the man to be a bigoted misogynist,' Clare said.

'Misogynist? Do you think he was?'

'If what Cheryl Milledge said is true, his attempting to take advantage on a stage in front of an audience, then I'd say he was.'

'You're sure that he wasn't a closet deviant, and she represented an object of lust.'

'Trevor Winston called him repressed. Maybe Mason was unable to make it with a woman and was relegated to prostitutes.'

'There's no record of her selling herself,' Tremayne said.

'I'm aware of that.'

'And we know that Fiona Dowling is probably no better.'

'But she's married, refined. Considering the two women went to school together, it's hard to see two more dissimilar women.'

'It still doesn't solve the reason why Mason was murdered, and it needed two people or one person and two daggers.'

'Or if he visited prostitutes.'

'It's possible he didn't, and if he did, he'd want to keep it secret.'

'Someone was blackmailing him?'

'If they were, it would be him killing them, not the other way around,' Tremayne said. 'We need to find out the truth about Pearson and the lovely Fiona Dowling.'

'Is that how you see her?'

'Not really. I prefer Cheryl Milledge. Earthy, that's what Dennison called her, an apt description. She's an open book. What you see is what you get, no airs and graces,' Tremayne said.

'You wouldn't want her cleaning your house.'

'I can do that badly enough without her assistance, thank you very much. If I gave you half a chance, Yarwood, you'd be there making me run around with a mop and a bucket of water.'

'You're right there, guv.'

'Not a chance. Let's go and find out about this affair.'

'Southampton?'

'No. Let's make Fiona Dowling sweat.'

'It's probably the only motive so far that's strong enough to justify murder.'

'It's good enough, that's for sure.'

***

As assumed, Fiona Dowling was busy, ready to go out. To Clare, it seemed that the woman always wanted to portray activity and importance. Clare was sure that she was addicted to the smartphone she clutched in her hand, its gold case clearly visible.

'I can't give you long. I'm meeting up with some friends. We're organising a charity drive for the school.'

'Are you involved with lots of worthwhile causes, Mrs Dowling?' Tremayne asked. Clare could see that the man was not going to let her get out of giving him a straight answer.

'I see it as my civic duty.'

'Don't you help your husband with his business?'

'I've done my fair share. We set it up together, not a penny between us. I've told you that.'

'Commendable, I'm sure,' Tremayne said. 'I suggest you cancel your meeting. Some questions need answering.'

'Why me?'

'You were at Old Sarum, you saw the man stabbed.'

'I was around the back. I didn't see it. I heard it, that's all.'

'We have one important question for which we need an answer.'

'Give me two minutes. I'll delay my meeting for an hour.' Fiona Dowling took out her phone and made several phone calls. 'One hour, is that sufficient?'

'It should be,' Clare said.

'What do you want to know?'

'We don't have a reason for the man's murder. We're certain that two people are responsible. There may be some conjecture there, but at least one person wanted him dead,' Tremayne said.

'Why on a stage?'

'The sense of the theatrical?' Clare said. She realised that it was a valid point that the woman had raised.

'Sergeant Yarwood is probably right. The ultimate accolade – to commit murder in front of a live audience,' Tremayne said.

'But no one knows who it was,' Fiona Dowling said.

'That's as maybe, so why do it if there is no acknowledgement? Do actors suffer from self-doubt, the inability to believe in themselves, the need to convince themselves that they are the best, even if others don't think so?'

'You don't know actors, Detective Inspector. They're full of self-doubt and neuroses. Gordon Mason barely said two civil words off stage, but up there, he's extrovert, pawing the females, projecting his voice.'

'Pawing?'

'Yes. He tried it with me, but I made it clear enough that if he got too close, I'd scream blue murder and have him up in front of the local magistrate. And yes, I know about Cheryl and Mason.'

'What do you mean?' Clare asked.

'On the stage when he became excited.'

'Outside of there?'

'I wouldn't put it past her. She'd be game for anything.'

'That's a damning indictment.'

'I've nothing against the woman personally. We were the best of friends once, but now we have little in common.'

'Is she an intelligent woman?'

'Cheryl, very. She was certainly smarter than me, but she didn't have the drive. It's not the best who make it, it's the most determined. You must know that.'

I'm determined to crack this case wide open,' Tremayne said.

'What is it you want to know?'

'We are led to believe that you are having an affair with Geoff Pearson,' Clare said.

'What, are you joking? Who made such a scurrilous statement? I'll take legal action.'

Clare could see that the woman was taken aback. Her protestations were a clear sign of guilt.

'We have a strong belief that this is correct,' Tremayne said.

'It can't be. I'm faithful to my husband, a good mother.'

'We're not here to judge, and this is confidential if it does not pertain to the murder enquiry.'

'My position? What if people find out about this lie?'

'If it's a lie, what does it matter?'

'You know it matters. The people I associate with thrive on gossip.'

'You do as well, would that be correct, Mrs Dowling?' Clare said.

'I suppose so. It's harmless.'

'You also had a past in your youth that you'd prefer no one to know about.'

'I admitted that to you before. I was young and into one-night stands, but that was a long time ago.'

'Would your friends understand, your committees?'

'Most of them have a past. That wouldn't be an issue.'

'But an affair would?' Tremayne said.

'An affair, yes. Some of them would shun me, tell Len. My life would be hell.'

'Is it true? We will find out.'

'Who told you?'

'Does it matter?'

'Was it Geoff?'

'Our source does not matter. The truth is important.'

Fiona Dowling sat down and closed her eyes. Clare could see that the woman who had portrayed herself as one of the doyennes of the social set was in turmoil.

'Sometimes, I feel the need. You don't understand how hard it is pretending all the time, always making sure that I'm dressed correctly, the hair and the makeup are perfect.'

'Then why do you do it?' Clare asked.

'Why, you ask me why I put up with some of those stuck-up bitches on their church committees? I'll tell you why. Because I can. I grew up with Cheryl, spoke like her, screwed around like her, but I wanted more. I fought for what I have, dragged Len along with me. And, believe me, back then he was a whimpering fool, ambitious but clueless. I made him what he is today.'

'Why the affair?'

'You don't understand, do you?'

'Not really,' Clare said.

'You're still young and pretty. I'm getting old. I need to be loved.'

'You have a husband.'

'He's getting old as well. I need more. I need a young man, virile and strong. I need Geoff Pearson. Is that enough for you?'

'That's fine,' Clare said. 'We'll leave you alone now.'

'Are you satisfied?' Fiona Dowling asked.

'Satisfied? We're police officers, not arbiters of morality. We deal in facts only. Unless it is vital, what you have told us here today will remain confidential.'

'I hope it does. You don't know how it feels to get old, to not turn a man's head.'

Outside the house, Tremayne turned to Clare. 'That woman has got enough neuroses for all of the Salisbury Amateur Dramatic Society.'

'And some. She's not much older than me.'

'She's a woman who could hate.'

'Murder?'

'She'd be capable if it was to protect her perfect life.'

'Do you call that perfect?'

'Give me Cheryl Milledge any time. At least she's good for a pint and a laugh. With Fiona Dowling, I'd be forever treading on eggshells.'

'Len Dowling must know what he's got. He can't be that naïve.'

'We'll need to interview him again. We'll not bring up the affair, of course.'

'It's bound to come out sometime.'

'It may have already. I wouldn't have thought that Cheryl, for all her good points, is the sort of person to keep a secret indefinitely.'

'A motive for murder?'

'Without a doubt. The woman would murder to keep it quiet.'

'Or Gordon Mason may have found out about it, threatened her.'

'Money?'

'Not money. The man was desperate. He would have enjoyed forcing Fiona Dowling to have sex with him to protect her secret, the ultimate misogynist's degradation.'

'What happened to a good old husband beats wife, wife kills husband murder?' Clare said.

'You'd be bored within a day. This case has legs. We just need to wind up the suspects.'

'All ten?'

'All of them. Who's next?' Tremayne said.

Clare could see why Tremayne liked Cheryl Milledge, they were both open books. What you see is what you get.

Chapter 10

Tremayne and Clare waited outside the Dowlings' house for twenty minutes. Fiona Dowling came out of the front door, slamming it shut. She then opened the driver's seat of her Range Rover and drove off.

'The woman doesn't give up, does she?' Tremayne said.

'She's even fixed her makeup. She intends to continue relentlessly, no matter what was just said,' Clare said.

'I always thought that Len Dowling was the driven one, but apparently it's her.'

'It could be both. She's not the sort of woman to give credit to others.'

'It's strange that everyone is willing to offer a comment about Cheryl Milledge, yet it's her friend who is much worse.'

'How do we find out if Mason was pressuring her?'

'Bank account records.'

'The woman doesn't look short of cash, judging by the house and the car.'

'Can an estate agency make that much?'

'It probably does well enough, but they may have investments.'

'Dodgy deals?'

'Some of those. We can ask Fraud to check out Dowling.'

'What's for us?'

'Samantha Dennison,' Clare said.

'Why her?'

'She's a mercenary woman and a hater.'

'She's not the murderer.'

'She'd know the dirt, especially if her husband had told her. I doubt if she's discreet either. She can fill us in on the background of the others. It may help.'

'You know the address.'

'I'm driving, is that it?'

'Yarwood, you'll make a great detective inspector. I can see the sixth sense there.'

'Just because I figured out that you're too lazy to drive.'

'That's it, and besides, I need to check the form for tomorrow.'

'You mean which horse should win, and the day after, why it lost.'

'Just drive, no potholes either.'

'Yes, Detective Inspector.'

Samantha Dennison was at home when they arrived. Clare had taken the precaution to phone ahead.

'Where's your husband?' Clare asked once they were inside the house.

'He's got a place at the end of the garden; his den, as he calls it.'

'What does he do there?'

'That's where he conducts his business. Unless it's vital, I'm not allowed there.'

'Harsh,' Tremayne said.

'It doesn't concern me. Let him have his little secrets if that's what he wants.'

'Mrs Dennison, we need to know about your secrets.'

'Why? I wasn't there when that man died.'

'We're aware that you're not involved. It's just that you were there once, your husband had a run-in with Mason, and you've probably got a good eye for people.'

'If you mean I'm nosy?'

'Not at all. You're an impartial observer. Everyone we've interviewed so far could have a vested interest, could even be the murderer.'

'Including Phillip?'

'It's possible,' Tremayne said.

'What do you want to know?'

'The one time you went to one of their productions. What can you tell us?'

'It was a rehearsal. It was Phillip, he was keen to show me what he got up to, or to convince me that he wasn't playing up with one of the women.'

'Was that likely?'

'You've seen me, you've seen Phillip.'

'What are you getting at?'

'I'm not under any illusions, are you?'

'He's an older man,' Clare said.

'As you're the police and you can check me out, it's better if I tell you. Phillip plays the financial markets in a big way. The man has an ego that allows him to take risks. I have to admire him for that. That ego needs feeding.'

'And?'

'I'm part of the ego. Don't get me wrong. I know what I am, what other people see me as, especially that Mason. He looked me up and down, had me stripped naked there in front of his beady eyes, trying to look down my cleavage.'

'You must have come across that before. You're not a shrinking violet,' Clare said.

'I don't make a pretence. I set out to snare Phillip, I don't intend to let him go.'

'And the women at the dramatic society?'

'There was one, a bit rough around the edges. I didn't mind her nor her layabout boyfriend. The man in charge, what was his name?'

'Peter Freestone,' Clare said.

'Yes, that's him. He was polite, as was the funeral director, although he wasn't a cheerful person, the job I suppose, looking at dead bodies every day. The young kid fancied his chances, and Trevor Winston, he's a good hairdresser and certainly not interested in me. He would have fancied the young kid, given half a chance.'

'Jimmy Francombe's not homosexual,' Clare said.

'He's tried to chat you up?'

'He's tried.'

'He's got plenty of nerve, I'll give him that. I couldn't get rid of him.'

'Was that an issue?' Tremayne asked.

'Not really. The boy was harmless, and he behaved himself, not like some others.'

'Mason?'

'He sees me walk in the door, pretending to turn up his nose, made some disparaging comments about me to the others.'

'What sorts of comments?'

'I couldn't hear, but I can tell you what they were: old man's fancy, gold digger, tart, hawking herself for an old man's money. I've heard it all before.'

'Does it upset you?'

'Sometimes. It's not all true. I'm fond of Phillip, the same he is of me. He's a few years older than me and lonely, I was poor and attractive. Please, that's not false modesty. I'm honest as to what I am, how men see me, especially men like Phillip who've spent a lifetime chasing money, failing to settle down, bring up a family. I'm the substitute reward, although what he really wants is to relive his life, the same as everyone else, but it's too late for him.'

'Too late for you?' Clare asked.

'I'm not wired that way. I'm not into domesticity and children. If it's not Phillip, I'll find someone else, until I'm old and no longer desirable.'

'And then?'

'Retire to a convent,' Samantha Dennison said.

'Would you?' Tremayne asked.

'Not likely. I've got a small house in the Caribbean. I'll move there and surround myself with animals, the eccentric old woman in the house up the end of the road.'

'What were you doing before you met your husband?'

'I was working in an office, being ogled by the manager, pawed by the office boy if he got half a chance, squeezing me against the photocopier. One day, Phillip comes in, we get talking. Three months later we were married on a beach in Antigua.'

'You've been honest with us,' Tremayne said.

'I've no reason not to be. I've done nothing wrong. I've made Phillip happy; he's made me happy. Is there anything else in life?'

Clare wanted to say the unconditional love between two people but decided not to.

'What can you tell us about Geoff Pearson. You've met him, I suppose.'

'The university student?'

'That's him,' Clare said.

'He was polite, but he wasn't interested in me.'

'Why not?'

'He's screwing the estate agent's wife. Sorry about the language, but that's the truth.'

'How do you know this?'

'I've got two eyes. I could see them making sure to avoid eye contact, and in the rehearsal, when he has to hold her, he's not holding her tight, pretending to be impassive.'

'Did anyone see this?'

'If they did, they never mentioned it.'

'You deduced that they were involved purely by observation.'

'I was the impartial observer. I picked it up straight away.'

'You've told your husband.'

'I've told no one, only you.'

'What did you make of Len Dowling, the estate agent?'

'Not much. He sounds off a lot, but there's not much substance. Geoff Pearson doesn't say much, but he's certainly getting on with it, at least with that woman.'

'You didn't like her?'

'I saw through her. The affected accent, the mannerisms.'

'You saw that?'

'A kindred spirit, competition under different circumstances.'

'You were hard on your husband the last time we were here,' Tremayne said.

'He thrives on it. I act like a bitch, but that's what he wants. He wants to be dominated.'

84

Clare did not believe the woman. Samantha Dennison was, by her own admission, a gold digger. By Clare's definition, a bitch.

'We've not discussed Gordon Mason in detail,' Tremayne said.

'He told Phillip what he thought of me, not that it stopped him undressing me. Phillip reacted, pushed Mason to one side, causing the man to fall over.'

'What did the others say or do?'

'It was outside. I don't think anyone saw it.'

'And your reaction?'

'I kicked the man on the ground.'

'What did Mason do?'

'He swore, called me a whore. Phillip didn't see that. We left soon after. Phillip was upset for a while, but I calmed him down.'

'How?' Clare asked.

'You're a smart woman, you figure it out.'

'Thank you for your time, Mrs Dennison. If your husband asks, we were just following up on our enquiries.'

'I'll not tell him. He's in his own little world down there.'

***

Fiona Dowling attended the all-important meeting with her social friends, even conducted herself in her typical effusive manner. Once free of them, she was on the road.

Geoff Pearson was surprised to see her outside in the street when his last lecture for the day concluded. 'Fiona, what are you doing here?'

'The police. They know about us.'

'How?'

'I never told them. Who else knows about us?'

'We were always discreet, careful where we met, and you being here doesn't help. You could be seen.'

'In Southampton? Get real, Geoff, I can't afford to lose Len, nor you. I need you both.'

'One to provide you with the money, the other to satisfy you,' Pearson said.

'I made Len what he is, you know that.'

'Yes, and you'd have me jumping through the same hoop if you had half a chance.'

'You've never loved me, it's true, isn't it?'

'Fiona, you've always known what it was. I'm a struggling student, you're a bored housewife. It's been fun, still is, but don't get carried away.'

'I trusted you, and you told the police.'

'I never told them, that's the honest truth. Others have suspected, but I've never admitted to anything,' Pearson said, knowing full well that Cheryl had seen them that one time and Gary Barker knew as well.

'You've got to do something.'

'What do you want me to do? The police suspect that we're having an affair. There's no proof.'

'I admitted it to them. I was flustered, they were determined, and I needed to get out of the house.'

'You stupid, stupid woman. Don't you know anything? Always deny. What do you think Len will say when he hears about this? He'll divorce you, take away your car and your house, even claim custody of the children.'

'I love you, Geoff. I want to be with you. He can't take the house and the car, they're in my name.'

'Why?'

'Tax avoidance. It's legitimate, sort of, and besides, he'll not divorce me. The man's weak without me, but I need you, I love you.'

Geoff Pearson could see difficulties, difficulties he did not want. He was a man destined for greatness; he did not need a clingy and neurotic woman. He needed to get rid of her. 'Fiona, this can't continue. You need to go back to Len, beg his forgiveness if it comes out, but you can't rely on me.'

'What was I, just another screw? I was better than all those young girls you take out, more mature, more able to guide your career, your life.'

Pearson was panicking, he knew it. It had been fun, the older woman, the meetings at the out-of-town hotels, the back of the Range Rover with the seats folded down, but now the situation was serious. He had exams coming up, a potential new girlfriend in his year at university. He no longer needed the distraction, although when they had first made love, one night after rehearsals when she had given him a ride home in her car, it had been fun, and Fiona, he had known, was lacking the attention that she needed.

Then it had been a bit on the side for her, a substantial boost to his male prowess, but now she was in love, desperate love, and he did not want it. 'Sorry, Fiona, it was fun, but it's over. I wish you well, but that's it.'

Pearson left the car and walked, almost ran, away from the scene. Fiona, heartbroken but still resolute, spoke to herself: *You bastard, you'll pay for this.*

She then turned the ignition key of her car and pulled out from where she had been parked. She wiped her tears away with the sleeve of her blouse.

Chapter 11

Clare, feeling better than she had for a long time, joined Tremayne for a drink. This time, the Bridge Inn in the Woodford Valley. It wasn't the first time they had been there; the last time she had been drinking whisky.

Tremayne remembered that night well, the clouds, the roar of thunder, the lightning over Mavis Godwin's cottage, but neither of the police officers wanted to discuss that case: too many unpleasant memories, especially for Clare.

Tremayne had a pint of beer in his hand, Clare was sticking to orange juice.

'What do you reckon, Yarwood?' Tremayne asked.

'The motives to kill the man are not strong. I can understand their dislike, but murder hardly seems justified. For sure, Fiona Dowling's a case, what with her airs and graces, butter wouldn't melt in her mouth attitude, but she's more concerned with her place in society. Languishing behind bars wouldn't suit her image.'

'Samantha Dennison?'

'The woman was refreshingly honest. She made no attempt to conceal what she was, what her husband was. She might fleece a man for his money, but there's no percentage in murder, and besides, she wasn't at Old Sarum.'

'The perfect alibi.'

'But why would the others have wanted Mason dead?'

'This angle on him blackmailing Fiona Dowling? Do you give it any credence?'

'It's a possibility.'

'Geoff Pearson, her accomplice?'

'Only if she had had a chance to knife Mason, and then that's hit and miss. What if Pearson had missed the heart on stage? Mason would still be conscious, and he wouldn't have lain down still.'

'And remember Mark Antony had time on the stage, the Senate scene where Brutus and his fellow conspirators leave to address the mob. Mason wasn't moving then, and Mark Antony, or should I say Phillip Dennison, did not have a chance to stab him. The man was dead on that stage after the conspirators had stabbed him. I'm discounting Dennison, the same as I'm discounting the women.'

'Then you believe it's two of the conspirators,' Clare said.

'Peter Freestone is an accountant, serves as a city councillor, and Len Dowling's an estate agent.'

'Too predictable: a rezoning, privileged information, buying up land for a steal, selling it on afterwards.'

'We're not looking for the obscure here, just the murderers.'

'Freestone and Dowling were both on stage, both had a clear target. It could be them, but we never checked how far Mason staggered after the main assault. If there were thirty-three stabs before the final stab of Freestone's, then four would have penetrated his body, one of them at least in his heart.'

'How do we find out?'

'We can't ask the actors in case of collusion.'

'Yarwood, you interviewed the audience, took names and addresses. We'll need to talk to them.'

'I'll set it up.'

'In the meantime, I'll have another pint. Are you sticking to that orange juice?'

'Someone needs a clear head.'

***

'We often go to one of their productions. They're not bad for amateurs.' Tremayne and Clare were standing in a warehouse on the outskirts of the city. Derek Wilkinson, the manager of the wholesale electrical supplier, was a man with similar tastes in clothing to Tremayne, judging by his tie off to one side, his shirt marked with a felt pen. To Clare, the two men were similar in looks as well, apart from the fact that Tremayne was well over six feet and Wilkinson was a short man, almost dwarfish.

'We were there, but there's one crucial scene that we're unsure of,' Clare said.

'Ask away. It was a shame that it ended suddenly. Poetic, I suppose.'

'What do you mean?'

'No disrespect for the dead, but it was meant to be a play, fake daggers, fake blood, a fake death, and there is Gordon Mason dead on the floor.'

'Did you know the man?'

'In passing. I can't say I liked him, but he was competent, honest as well.'

'And some are not?'

'Not really, but you always hear stories about solicitors and estate agents, city councillors.'

'Have you heard about any of those recently?' Tremayne asked.

'Not recently.'

'In the past?'

'There was a subdivision, about a dozen blocks of land that had been zoned industrial.'

'What happened?'

'I was looking for somewhere to build this warehouse, and the price was reasonable. At the rear, there was a floodplain.'

'What happened?'

'It was rezoned residential, the price shot up. Not that it did any good for those who built their houses there.'

'What do you mean?'

'You remember when it rained solidly for two weeks, a few years back?'

'I remember,' Tremayne said.

'Half of the houses were flooded out, the insurance companies rejected their claims, said it was an act of God. Serves them right.'

'Why do you say that?'

'A good solicitor, a few checks, would have found out about the potential of flooding.'

'Who was the solicitor?'

'For the vendor, or for the purchaser?'

'Either.'

'Len Dowling sold the land. Joint ownership with his brother, he's a solicitor.'

Tremayne looked at Clare: a motive.

'Let's get back to the play,' Tremayne said.

'What do you want to know?' Wilkinson asked.

'When Caesar staggered over to Brutus.'

'I remember it.'

'Did he stagger?'

'It wasn't far, but yes, he staggered.'

'How far?'

'Six feet, maybe eight.'

'And then, did he utter *Et tu, Brute*?'

'It was weak, but yes, I heard him say it.'

'Thanks. That's all we need to know.'

'A motive that holds up,' Tremayne said to Clare once they were outside the warehouse.

'It still raises more questions,' Clare said.

'Such as?'

'If someone is stabbed in the heart, or in the body, it can't be guaranteed that they will still be able to stagger. The man could easily have collapsed on the spot.'

'The dramatic effect would have been lost, but the man would still have been dead.'

'And if he were, then Peter Freestone would never have had a chance to stick his dagger in, no immortal line from Caesar.'

'Are you saying that Freestone's not guilty?'

'He could still be guilty, but it's illogical. You have two lethal weapons, why would you leave it to chance to use the second one?'

'Are we discounting Freestone as one of the murderers?'

'I think we are,' Clare said. 'We're assuming that he was involved in a possible fraudulent rezoning, and maybe he was, but he's not one of the murderers.'

'I'll make a good police officer out of you yet, Yarwood,' Tremayne said. 'I thought we had the case sewn up in there, but now it's obvious that it's still wide open.'

***

With the preliminary interviews concluded, the most potent motive was that Peter Freestone, Len Dowling, and Dowling's brother had been involved in a fraudulent land deal. And that Gordon Mason had knowledge of the fraud, either through involvement or through investigation, and the man was about to reveal what he knew. The weakest motive was that Trevor Winston had objected to the treatment meted out in rehearsals, and Mason's continuing bias against him because of his sexual orientation. The other motives, the blackmailing of Fiona Dowling for sexual favours or for money, seemed a long shot, but yet again the two police officers were clutching at straws.

Tremayne was sure there was more depth to the motives. Clare was not sure how to proceed. The one interview she did not want her and Tremayne to conduct was with Len Dowling's brother, Chris. She knew the day would come when she'd have to confront a return to Harry's old pub, or next door, which was where Chris Dowling had an office, on the first floor.

'If you'd rather not,' Tremayne said, but Clare knew that was not possible. She was a police officer, not a schoolgirl crying over being dumped by her boyfriend; she was a mature woman, rapidly becoming an experienced homicide detective, not that Tremayne said so, but then she knew the man gave compliments sparingly.

She was aware that he was looking to her, not only as a sounding board for his analysis of the case, the direction to move forward, but also to bring new ideas into the discussion, and she had. She had been the one who had seen the possibility that Peter Freestone, the last assassin up at Old Sarum, could not have been one of the murderers, and if that was the case, then the motive of the suspected rezoning fraud may not be correct. Regardless, it wouldn't be the first time that murder had been committed over money.

If Clare's preliminary checks were accurate then the change from industrial to rezoning had increased the value of the land from half a million pounds sterling to two million pounds sterling, and the owner before and after, Len Dowling. The necessary legal ownership had been dealt by Chris Dowling, and the city council meeting where the decision had been made for the rezoning chaired by Peter Freestone. Gordon Mason's involvement was not so clear, as the council had their own legal team, and the change from industrial to residential was an internal matter.

Minster Street was busy as Tremayne and Clare walked down it. They had parked their car in the Guildhall Square and walked past the Poultry Cross, another ancient building, before turning right towards Chris Dowling's office.

Clare looked at the pub, Harry's pub, their pub, as she had loved it as much as he had. She saw the first-floor window of the room where they had made love. Even imagined the cellar where the beer barrels were stored, and where they had almost made love that first time, only to be interrupted by the anxious patrons upstairs, and then the gentle rebuke from Tremayne about the buttons on her blouse being undone.

'Doesn't do to dwell on the past, Yarwood,' Tremayne said in his typically blunt manner.

Clare knew that the man cared, even if he wouldn't admit to it, and since the events in Avon Hill his choice of favoured pub varied from night to night; sometimes he had even spent a quiet evening at home.

They were ushered into Chris Dowling's office by an efficient woman who asked them to sign a book on her desk recording times in and out before she opened the door to the solicitor's office to let him know that they had arrived.

'Come in, please,' Chris Dowling said. Clare could see that he bore no similarity to his brother.

'We're here investigating the death of Gordon Mason.'

'Tea, coffee, Detective Inspector, Sergeant?'

'I'll have tea, milk, two sugars,' Tremayne said.

'No sugar for me, thank you,' Clare said.

'What can I do for you? Gwyneth will only be a minute with the tea.'

'Your brother, Len, said that you handle all his legal work.'

'Step-brother, but yes, that's true.'

'Not far from here, off Churchfields Road, there was some land that was rezoned from industrial to residential.'

'It happens from time to time.'

'Only this time, the guidelines relating to the floodplain were ignored. Subsequently, some houses were flooded.'

'Are you saying this was a possible motive for Mason's murder?'

'If there was fraud, then your brother, and possibly Peter Freestone, stood to gain.'

'And me. I've a twenty per cent interest in Len's business.'

Clare could see that the two brothers were not alike in mannerisms either: one was loud and extrovert, the other was careful in what he said, not wishing to incriminate, not wanting to make a firm denial of anything untoward. She was not sure which of the two she preferred, or even if she liked either. Len Dowling was a salesman, his brother was possibly devious, and if there had been something underhand, the man would have covered their tracks well.

'You are aware of the land in question?' Tremayne said.

'It may be best if you do your research before you come here, Detective Inspector.'

'Why?' Tremayne said. Clare could sense the atmosphere becoming frosty.

'At the time of the flooding, some of the residents contacted the local newspaper. There was an article in there, a subsequent special meeting held in the council chambers. In the end, the council agreed to put in place measures to prevent another flood, and compensated all of the affected houses with a rates reduction.'

'That doesn't alter the fact that the rezoning may have been fraudulent.'

'Heavy words, legally prejudicial against my brother and myself, not to mention Peter Freestone and the other members of the Salisbury City Council,' Dowling said. Tremayne sat quietly, taking in the man who had gone from pleasant to aggressive in no more than a few minutes.

'Mr Dowling, I believe that your attitude is counter-productive,' Tremayne said. 'We did not come here to be confrontational, we never accused anyone of any wrongdoing. A man has been murdered. It is for us to follow up on any innuendo regardless. If, as I infer by your attitude, you are threatening us with legal action if we persist, then you should think again.'

'Very well, but I should warn you that I team up with Superintendent Moulton at the golf club out on Netherhampton Road every Saturday afternoon.'

Clare visibly sat back at Dowling's oblique threat.

'Mr Dowling, with all due respect, you could be teaming up with the Almighty, it does not impact on the fact that Sergeant Yarwood and I are conducting a murder enquiry. Our visit here today, our questioning of you, is within our rights as police officers. I suspect that you have not been involved in a murder enquiry before, I have, and Superintendent Moulton will not interfere with how I run this investigation. Now, getting back to our previous questioning. What do you know about the rezoning of this land? Did anyone benefit financially?'

Dowling did not speak for several minutes. Tremayne knew the man wasn't used to being put in his place. 'Len benefited,' Dowling finally said.

'Who else?'

'Apart from the additional revenue to the city council, no one.'

'The rezoning application, did you prepare the submission?'

'Yes, but it was all above board. We brought in an expert, well-respected in his field, who said the chance of flooding was a once in a one-hundred-year event.'

'What happened?'

'Three years after the last house there had been completed, we had the one-hundred-year flood. It probably won't happen again, at least not in our lifetimes.'

'Any payments to Peter Freestone?'

'None. I ensured the necessary council fees were paid, that was all.'

'And Gordon Mason?'

'He acted on behalf of some of the purchasers, nothing more.'

'Thank you, Mr Dowling. We've no further questions.'

Tremayne and Clare left the office without their cups of tea.

'What do you reckon, Yarwood?' Tremayne asked.

'I didn't like him.'

'A slimy individual, worse than the brother.'

'Was there any illegal activity?'

'With the rezoning, almost certainly. It still doesn't tie in Mason.'

'We don't know if he was involved, or just became aware of it, threatened to take action, or was blackmailing them for other reasons.'

'The motive is strong, even if unproven. We'll need to keep a watch on Solicitor Dowling. Estate agent Dowling's not as sharp as that man.'

Chapter 12

Jim Hughes was in the office on Tremayne and Clare's return to the office. 'I've been working with Forensics on the daggers.'

'Any luck?'

'Some. The retractable daggers are an exact copy of an original that was discovered fifty years ago in an archaeological dig in Rome.'

'Does that help us?'

'It does. Up till then, the exact specifications were well known, but the look and feel were vague. Once this dagger had been found, some companies in the USA started making exact replicas. There's demand for knives, daggers, and swords around the world.'

'Here in England?' Tremayne asked.

'There are collectors here, although our laws are strict on the importation, unless they've been blunted or you're a registered collector.'

'Are there many collectors?'

'Not a lot.'

'In America?'

'They're easy to obtain there.'

'What are you telling us?'

'It would be possible to obtain metal blades in the USA and to change them with the plastic blades on the fakes.'

'Dimension, fitting into the retracting mechanism?' Tremayne asked.

'If an example was sent. Not too many questions would have been asked. We'll keep checking, but as I see it,' Hughes said, 'the person who purchased the fakes is probably not the person who purchased the metal blades.'

'How do we find out?' Clare asked.

'That's up to you. You're the investigators, but don't go looking for names. It's almost certainly an online transaction,

PayPal, maybe a bank transfer, but if someone were intent on murder, they'd have covered their tracks. Anyone smart enough?'

'There are several who spring to mind,' Tremayne said.

***

It was known that Peter Freestone, as the dramatic society's current president, had purchased the fake Roman daggers. The man had proof, and he had already stated that they had remained in his possession up until the staging of the play at Old Sarum.

Tremayne was willing to give Freestone the benefit of the doubt concerning his placing the fakes on a makeshift table at Old Sarum. If that was correct, then how were they changed, and by whom? It was Clare who suggested it first: a re-enactment.

Clare realised afterwards that getting everyone up there at the same time as the previous performance was not going to be that easy. For one thing, she needed the cooperation of the heritage society, then there was Len Dowling who was busy, Fiona, his wife, who was socialising, and Trevor Winston who was involved with the ladies in his salon.

Gary Barker and Cheryl Milledge were keen. 'Can we come in costume?' Cheryl asked.

'It's up to you,' Clare replied. She thought that it would have helped, but getting all the people there was one thing, getting the others in costume would have been nigh on impossible.

Geoff Pearson was reluctant, what with exams coming up, but Clare had leant on his good nature, not on an official summons. 'I'll be there,' he said. 'I wanted to avoid Fiona.'

'Lover's tiff?'

'You could say that. She's a vengeful woman. She could even tell Len out of spite.'

'Would she?' Clare said.

'With Fiona, who knows?'

'We'll be there. If there's an issue, we'll deal with it. We know about you and her.'

'She accused me of telling you.'

'She'd not believe you,' Clare said. 'You were playing with fire there.'

'It was fun for a while.'

'No guilt about her husband?'

'None. The man is not the type of person who'd garner respect from me.'

'Any reason?'

'No substance, no backbone. His wife screws around. Maybe he doesn't know about me, but there would have been others.'

'Would there?'

'What's your honest opinion of her?' Pearson asked.

Clare wasn't sure if she should divulge too much, but the man was talking, and he seemed to have his ear to the ground. 'Someone said that Cheryl Milledge is what you see, what you get.'

'It may have been me, not sure, but yes, with Cheryl, she's transparent. With Fiona, she's deep. I never knew when she was pretending or when she was honest.'

'You've broken up with her?'

'She came to Southampton; it got very nasty. Never trust her.'

'Could Mason have had some dirt on her?'

'She'd do anything to protect her reputation.'

'Murder?'

'I wasn't thinking of that, but she could be violent. I got out of her car fast before she started hitting me.'

'The scar on your face?'

'Not a woman. An accident as a child, that's all. I'm not a bastard, just a young guy indulging a fantasy.'

'The married, more mature woman?'

'Sergeant Yarwood, if you must know, she's a passionate woman.'

'Nymphomaniac?' Clare asked.

'Not far off. I've got a girlfriend down in Southampton. I hadn't intended to return to Salisbury for some time.'

'You need to be at Old Sarum.'

'I'll be there, maybe I'll bring the girlfriend.'

'If you want a catfight.'

'I'll take a chance.'

Clare realised that it had been an illuminating phone call, in that Geoff Pearson had revealed more about Fiona Dowling's nature. She knew that they needed to talk to Cheryl Milledge at some stage to see if there was more in her previous friend's background than they were aware of.

Phillip Dennison was willing to attend the re-enactment. Clare could hear his wife in the background, complaining. The woman had said that her husband needed to be bossed around, a defect in his personality. Clare thought that she was playing a dangerous game, and unless she had a sharp solicitor, she could find herself back in an office being pressed up against the photocopier by every young lothario.

Bill Ford was willing, although it was inconvenient, needed some rescheduling, but, as he said, the dead don't keep to any timetable, and he would be there.

Jimmy Francombe was excited to hear from Clare, wanting to know if the hot date was still on, maybe after the re-enactment. Clare had to admit that she liked the young man, good-natured, willing to have a joke at himself. He took her put-down in good heart. 'I'm still working on you,' he said.

'Goodbye, Jimmy, not a chance,' Clare said.

***

Gordon Mason's body was eventually released and sent to Bill Ford for burial. The funeral was held in a Baptist church close to Salisbury. A pastor conducted the ceremony, Peter Freestone made a speech praising the man's commitment to the dramatic society, another woman, identified as an older sister, spoke on behalf of the family. Everyone in the dramatic society attended. Cheryl Milledge was for once dressed sombrely, Gary Barker in a suit. Clare noticed that his hands were clean, and there was no dirt under his fingernails. Len Dowling had appeared agitated, wanting to message on his phone, only to have Fiona, dressed to the hilt with a large black hat, chastise him to put it away.

Trevor Winston sat with Jimmy Francombe and Geoff Pearson. Pearson was keeping a low profile, hoping to avoid a face-to-face confrontation with Fiona Dowling. Clare could see her furtive glances as she looked for him. He had positioned himself behind a pillar, arriving late, hoping to leave early. All seemed suitably sad at the passing of the man that no one had liked.

Tremayne remembered the last funeral he had attended: a detective inspector colleague of his, younger than him by a few years, who had suddenly keeled over when he had been at a crime scene. The diagnosis was a massive heart attack brought on by too many drinks, often with him, too many cigarettes, and too many hours. Tremayne had recollected, in the church watching the congregation, the pastor conducting the funeral, strict Baptist, that he was as guilty of all the offences that his colleague had indulged in. For a few minutes, in the tranquillity of the moment, he had promised to himself to turn over a new leaf: no more getting drunk, cigarettes down to ten a day, and a stiff walk around the block every morning. Once the service concluded, and they were out in the fresh air, he had taken out a packet of cigarettes and lit up. *To hell with it*, he'd thought.

Clare, observing her senior indulging his favourite pastime, apart from beer and horse racing, left him and walked around the churchyard. Mason was not to be cremated but buried in the graveyard next to the church. She looked back at the church, its similarities to the church in Avon Hill undeniable. She thought that within a few weeks, once the current case was wrapped up, she would visit Harry's grave in the church where the pagans had conducted their rituals.

Harry had never mentioned other relatives, but it appeared that there was an uncle who had surfaced in Salisbury two days after his death. Apparently, his solicitor had known about him and his family but had not been authorised to reveal the details unless Harry was dead.

The uncle had turned out to be a Christian, dismissive of Harry and his parents' foolish ways, fully cognisant of who and what they were. Clare had spoken to the uncle briefly. At least the man had had the civility to ask her opinion of a Christian burial; she had agreed, but she had not attended the funeral, the grief had been too raw, although now she wished she had.

A graveyard outside a church was too much for her; she walked away and out to the road. 'Sergeant Yarwood,' Geoff Pearson said.

'I'm surprised to see you here,' Clare said.

'I had to do the right thing. The man was not easy to get on with, but he was genuine enough.'

'And the dramatic society?'

'It's hard to say. Once we've completed the re-enactment, I'll move to Southampton on a longer-term basis.'

'Fiona Dowling?'

'I was wrong, no need to lecture me.'

'I'm a police officer. I only want to solve this case.'

'Look around. There's the murderer.'

Clare turned her head, could only see the dramatic society members, the pastor, and Mason's sister. 'It doesn't help. Has she seen you?'

'Fiona, she sees everything.'

'And her husband?'

'Who knows. I'll honour Mason here today, attend your re-enactment and then make myself scarce. Hopefully, Fiona will find someone else.'

'Young and virile.'

'Young, at least. If you'll excuse me, Fiona's heading this way. You can deal with her.' Pearson jumped into his car, a female in the passenger seat, and left at speed.

'He's a miserable bastard. Don't go falling for him,' Fiona Dowling said, the brim of her hat attempting to fall down over her face in the wind. She took hold of it and held it high with one hand.

'He's a witness to a murder. I've no need of him, and even if I did, he's too young.'

'He was a great lay, I'll give him that.'

'Was that all it was? Nothing else?'

'Why should it be? I need some excitement in my life.'

'And he was the excitement?'

'It was better than playing tennis.'

'Do you?'

'Play tennis? Of course I do. I'm on their committee.'

'Your husband's here. Aren't you concerned that he'll find out about Pearson?'

'I'll deal with it if it happens.'

'You're a hard woman, Mrs Dowling.'

'I'm determined, never let anything get in my way. If Len is not up to it, I'll find someone else.'

'What are you referring to?'

'Business, screwing, whatever.'

'Would you kill for your lifestyle?'

'I'd kill for my children, not for that. If I want the lifestyle, I just have to wiggle my arse, flash some cleavage.'

'The other day you were complaining about your age.'

'Some days down, some days up.'

'Any reason?'

'Self-doubt. We all suffer from it. It's not always easy maintaining the pretence.'

Clare wondered if there was something more, something medical, that could change a vain and driven woman into a killer.

***

Tremayne had not gained much from the funeral, apart from how easy it was for the dramatic society to pretend to have liked the man when apparently none of them did. Peter Freestone had admitted to a grudging respect for him as a solicitor, and as an actor, and Cheryl Milledge had said some kind words about him at the wake. The last wake, Tremayne remembered, had been awash with alcohol, but this was Baptist, and it was teetotal, not that it stopped Bill Ford reaching for a small flask hidden in the inside pocket of his suit.

'I need to keep myself warm while they're in the church,' he said to Tremayne when he had been spotted. 'Most times at a funeral, I'm out in the cold.'

Tremayne had no issues with the man imbibing; he wished he'd brought a stiff drink as well. He was not a churchgoer, he knew that, though he'd attended enough funerals in his time. If it weren't for the murder, he'd not be there at all. He had to admit to feeling a little out of it, almost the relative who receives an invite out of kindness but isn't expected to come. However, this was the first opportunity to see all the suspects gathered in one place; to see the interactions, endeavour to pick up the nuances, the gestures, differentiate between genuine and feigned friendship.

As he stood to one side, observing, he could see that Cheryl Milledge and Fiona Dowling had acted correctly: a warm hug on meeting, a complimenting of each other's attire, a willingness to sit next to each other on the church pew. Tremayne wasn't sure what to make of the two women. Len Dowling, once he had stopped fiddling with his phone, had spoken to the pastor, as well as to Mason's sister. His wife had circulated, even pausing to have a chat with Jimmy Francombe.

Phillip Dennison was there, the Aston Martin parked in a prominent position for everyone to admire, but his wife not present. 'She's out shopping again,' he said with a sigh of exasperation. Tremayne felt for the man, though he wasn't sure why he did. He remembered that his wife had been the opposite, excessively frugal, always looking for the bargain. He had tried to explain that even though he was a humble police officer, they weren't destitute, and it's not a bargain if you didn't want it in the first place.

'You'll never understand,' she had said, as if there was something that he didn't get. He wondered what it was with the disparate group in that church and its graveyard that he didn't get with them.

'Tremayne, have you figured out which one of us is the murderer?' Freestone said as he came over to him.

'You purchased the daggers?' Tremayne said.

104

'A company online, remarkably cheap.'

'Realistic?'

'Considering the price, they are.'

'Who took responsibility for them?'

'I did initially, although the others would take them home occasionally if they wanted. The ones I purchased were harmless. No doubt Dowling's children had fun with them.'

'You'd trust a child with them?'

'I wouldn't. I don't know about Dowling, he may have.'

'His wife?'

'Not sure about her. I'm not always sure what she's thinking.'

'What do you mean?'

'Nothing in itself. I'm not judging anyone.'

'We still think it's two murderers. Just a question, off the record.'

'With you, Tremayne?'

'With me.'

'You're never off duty.'

'The land on the floodplain. We've people checking whether it was above board.'

'Are you insinuating that there may have been graft and corruption?'

'It's been mentioned.'

'Mason thought there was.'

'Did he say anything, do anything?'

'He would have, but there was nothing to find. There was an expert opinion, a rezoning unanimously agreed to by a quorum of councillors, a sign-off from our building inspector.'

'Dowling would have made plenty of money.'

'No doubt he did, but that's down to his good judgement in buying the land overpriced and then changing the zoning. He was close to the wind financially on that one, but it set him up.'

'The submission was backed up by experts?'

'And our building inspector. He's not a man to be easily swayed.'

'And the councillors?'

'We make our decisions based on advice received.'

'And if the advice is incorrect?'

'That's why we have people working for the council, people who check these things. I'm an accountant. I can tell you if it's financially viable, the tax implications, but don't ask me about floodplains, how to put one brick on top of another.'

'You're not handy?'

'I can barely fix anything.'

'Is there anyone that can?'

'In the dramatic society?' Freestone asked.

'Yes.'

'No idea. Geoff Pearson is good with tools. He fixed up our backdrop once, started one of the cars after rehearsals when it had a flat battery. Apart from that, I wouldn't know. Any reason to ask?'

'Someone modified the two daggers.'

'Is that what you think happened?'

'Would you have known if they had been changed?'

'On the night? Up at Old Sarum? Probably not. I don't think any of us would have been looking too closely. We were all tense, worrying about our lines, listening to our cue.'

'Cheryl Milledge works for the council, doesn't she?' Tremayne said.

'In our building approvals department. You don't think…'

'I don't think anything. I just observe, ask questions, look for answers.'

Chapter 13

Tremayne organised a team to check into the land rezoning that appeared to be flawed. He liked Cheryl Milledge, earthy as she had been described by Phillip Dennison, and now she was possibly the one person who could have changed the documents that were presented to council, and as they had been approved, then the building inspector would have been in on the fraud too. He had no time for Dennison's wife, the gold digger as he saw her, but she was honest about what she was, her purpose in the marital arrangements with her husband. And besides, she had not been up at Old Sarum that night when Mason had died, a plus in her favour, Tremayne had to admit.

Apart from a couple of wins on the horses in the last couple of days, Tremayne realised not a lot was going his way. Superintendent Moulton, the honeymoon period over following the success of the previous murder enquiry, was back into his attempts to retire Tremayne. He knew what it was, an effort to bring the average age of the police force in Salisbury down; most of them already looked to him as though they were just out of school, but they weren't, he knew that. Moulton saw a modern computer-driven procedural force, always smiling, or at least that's what was shown on the posters erected on Bemerton Road, the latest public relations exercise to instil confidence in the force, to encourage others to join.

Tremayne's gut instinct told him that the death of Mason was only the calm before the storm, a hornets' nest prodded, its occupants restless, waiting for the opportunity to strike and inflict their wrath on their victims. Yarwood, he could see, was coming over to his style of policing, but she was still young, susceptible to Moulton and his ideas. He hoped he could convince her in the long term to stay strong, but he wouldn't be around forever, and she was still vulnerable. He could see in her face at times the fragility after her fiancé's death. He assumed that once she left work and was back in the cottage that she was renting, the memories would return to her. He wanted to help but knew he could not. The best he could do was to keep her busy.

Tremayne realised that he had been sitting in his office for forty-five minutes, reminiscing, thinking. Too long for him, he realised, and there was a time when he would not have been able to do that. He envied Yarwood her ability to be in the office first thing in the morning, wide-awake and bushy-tailed, ready for the day ahead, yet as he pulled himself up from his chair, he could feel a twinge in his hips, tenderness in both of his knees. He cast a glance at his reflection in the glass partitioning that separated his office from the larger office beyond. He looked for the tell-tale signs, the signs that stared back at him every day as he stood in front of his bathroom mirror: the thinning hair, the lines in his face that weren't there before, the marks of ageing. The glass partition, an imperfect surface, showed what his mirror did, and he did not like it. He had been willing to accept the ageing process as inevitable, and now it was on him and he was not sure how much longer it would be before health problems started to set in.

Some of his work colleagues had passed on, his brother had gone, as had a cousin, a couple of drinking pals, even the bookmaker at Salisbury Races, and that man had had every reason to live, seeing that he had taken enough of his money.

Tremayne sat down. He made a phone call. 'Jean, let's meet in the next couple of weeks, go away for the weekend.'

'If you like,' his ex-wife replied.

Tremayne put the phone down and walked out of the office, the pains in his body temporarily forgotten.

***

Clare had not expected to run into Samantha Dennison, and if she had known that she would be in Trevor Winston's hairdressing salon, she would not have gone in.

'Sergeant Yarwood,' said Samantha's voice from under a hairdryer.

'Mrs Dennison,' Clare said.

'Call me Samantha. Us girls have got to stick together.'

Clare was not sure what the 'us girls' referred to, but let it pass.

'I thought I'd see how good Trevor Winston is,' Clare said.

'Sergeant Yarwood.' The unmistakable voice of Trevor Winston, the flamboyant clothing, the effeminate walk in the salon, although not outside in the street. Which was as well, Clare thought, as there was a rough element in the city, the legacy of the army bases in the area, the large number of men from more deprived parts of the country who saw violence as a solution, prejudice as a way of life. An effeminate man would have suited them fine to exercise their frustrations.

'I could do with a quick wash, style. Can you fit me in?'

Clare realised that she may be placing herself in the hands of a murderer, but she did not believe that he was, and it was unlikely that he'd inflict injury in his salon.

'No worries, just sit down next to Samantha, and I'll be right over.'

Clare turned to Samantha Dennison. 'How long have you known Trevor?'

'Ever since that time Phillip dragged me along to the dramatic society's rehearsal. Trevor gave me a card, the only good thing to come out of that evening.'

'Is Trevor a murderer?' Clare asked, knowing full well that she was using Tremayne's technique of baiting, hoping to elicit a response.

'He's skilled with a pair of scissors, but killing someone, I don't think so, and why?'

'Everyone has reasons, even you.'

'Don't look at me, I wasn't there that night.'

'You don't go along, support your husband?'

'Why should I? I'm an open book, a rich man's trophy. I'm under no illusion, neither is he. I admitted this before to you and your detective inspector.'

Clare knew she had an unexpected opportunity to see if the woman would open up, though she wasn't sure if there was anything more to be gleaned from her. Clare had to admit as she sat alongside the woman that she was attractive, the object of many men's fancy, in that she wore her skirts high, her blouses tight, her lipstick red and applied with care.

Trevor Winston was in the background, discussing with his assistant, another gay man, what style they should give Clare. She had wanted to spend no more than thirty minutes in there, a quick wash and blow dry, and then out to follow up on the team checking out the land deal. She messaged the team to tell them she would be late; she then messaged Tremayne to let him know that she had inadvertently run into Dennison's wife, and she'd take the opportunity for some gentle prying.

Tremayne had smiled on reading the message. *She's learning*, he thought. It was a technique he had often used over a pint of beer. The formal interview resulted in considered answers, carefully thought out, but no scurrilous rumours, innuendos, no dirt. Tremayne knew that Dennison's wife would be into all three. He was pleased that Yarwood was with the woman. He was interested to hear the results.

'Who else did you speak to that night when Trevor gave you his card?' Clare asked Samantha.

'The men were friendly, apart from that bastard.'

'Gordon Mason?'

'Yes, him.'

'Were you upset when your husband told you that he'd been murdered?'

'Phillip, he came in at four in the morning, babbling about it.'

'What was your reaction?'

'At that time? Nothing, I wasn't interested.'

'Someone is murdered, and you show no interest?' Clare said.

'Why? Phillip's always threatening to do me in.'

'To kill you?'

'He's all mouth and trousers.'

'What does that mean?'

'All talk, no substance. You've not heard that saying before? Where have you been living?'

'Norfolk.'

The two women laughed. Clare warmed to the woman.

'They used it all the time where I grew up. Phillip's all boast, no substance. He can threaten, but he'll do nothing.'

'Can you be sure?' Clare asked.

'He's had plenty of provocation, and all he does is rant and rave, pace up and down, occasionally throw something down hard on the floor, but he's never touched me.'

'We've always seen your husband as benign.'

'He is, but he's got a temper. He hit Gordon Mason that time.'

'Would your husband be capable of murder?'

'Of Mason?'

'Of anyone.'

'I don't see it, but who knows what anyone is capable of. I grew up as the child of a devout family. I even took the pledge to remain a virgin until married.'

'Did you?'

'Hell, no. The young man was just on sixteen, I was fifteen. He never knew what hit him, nor did I.'

'After that?'

'I could have screwed for England.'

'And with your husband?'

'I'm faithful to him, not that he wants me much.'

'Why's that? You're a beautiful woman.'

'With Phillip, the same as other men, the pursuit is what they want, not the ownership. Before he made it rich, he drove an old bomb, now he drives an Aston Martin, or at least I do. And what do I hear? How much fun he had with the old bomb. He owns an Aston Martin, he wants a Roll Royce.'

'He's got you. Does he want to trade up?'

'Trade me in for a younger version, is that what you think? Of course he does, but I've got a sharp lawyer. If he tries it, I'll sue him for half his assets, and I'll win, mark my words.

And I'll take his precious Aston Martin, even the Rolls Royce, and he knows it.'

'A good enough reason for murder,' Clare said.

'Of me, yes.'

'Would he?'

'Phillip, I'm not worried about him. All mouth and trousers, I told you that.'

'But he laid out Gordon Mason.'

'He hit him, but not that hard. I had my leg out behind him. The man fell hard, banged his head on the road, nothing more. Don't tell Phillip, he thinks he was the macho man defending his wife's honour.'

'You're not all mouth and trousers,' Clare said.

'I'm a mean bitch who says it as it is. I neither liked nor disliked Gordon Mason. I love my husband conditionally because he treats me well, let's me buy lots of trinkets.'

'And if he didn't?'

'I'd find another man. I've told you all this before. Think what you want of me. Phillip knows this.'

'Would you be capable of murder?'

'I wasn't at Old Sarum when the man died.'

'Hypothetically?'

'If my life was being threatened. If my children, assuming I had any, then yes, I could kill, and I'd have no guilt.'

'Would you have killed Gordon Mason if he had persisted with his derision?'

'That night he insulted me? Not a chance. If Phillip hadn't pushed him, and if Mason had come too close, I'd have kneed him in the groin, slapped him across the face.'

Trevor Winston came over, too early for Clare. 'How are you, ladies? A glass of champagne?'

'I'll have one,' Samantha said.'

'So will I,' Clare said. The woman was talking, she did not want her to stop.

'Sergeant, you're an attractive woman, why do you mess around playing cops and robbers? You could snare a man, enjoy life.'

'I had a man.'

'What happened?'

'He died.' Clare did not want to elaborate.

'Then get another one.'

'It doesn't work that way with me.'

'Idealistic, is that it? I was once, thought I'd get married, have a few children, and live the sweet life in the country.'

'What happened?'

'I wised up. In another ten years, the looks will have faded, and then it'll be hard.'

'That will happen to you.'

'I know that. That's why I've got a sharp lawyer and a place in the Caribbean.'

'Are you content, living the life that you do?' Clare asked.

'Are you?' Samantha Dennison asked.

'Not totally.'

'Neither am I, but with me, I'll be able to make the best of it. With you, it's work until you're in your sixties, then retirement in a place that you can barely afford, looking for the bargains in the supermarket. If my life is not perfect, it's better than yours.'

'We'll agree to disagree,' Clare said. She had to admit that although life was not good at the present time, it had been with Harry. She was sure that there would not be another man in her life. For the first time in several days, she felt sad.

'All done, Sergeant Yarwood,' Trevor Winston said.

Clare looked in the mirror; it was a vast improvement on when she had come in, but no one would appreciate it. Samantha Dennison had someone, even if it was not love, but Clare knew she did not envy the woman her superficial life.

Clare left the woman still being pampered and continued with her police work.

Chapter 14

Tremayne met Peter Freestone at the Pheasant Inn on the corner of Salt Lane and Rollestone Street. It was only a ten-minute walk for Freestone, and there was parking opposite for Tremayne. The pub was five hundred years old and wearing its age well. The half-timbered inn, a reminder of the time of Shakespeare and Elizabeth the first. Tremayne liked the pub, thought that it may become his favourite now the Deer's Head had closed.

Freestone was already seated in the corner closest to the fire on Tremayne's arrival. He had purchased two pints of beer: one for him, one for Tremayne.

'I've ordered a steak for both of us,' Freestone said.

'Fine,' Tremayne said. 'I thought we should get together before the re-enactment, run through some of the finer points.'

'Is there any suspicion that I'm involved?'

'It's a murder enquiry. I can't exonerate you just on the basis that we have the occasional pint together.'

'I understand,' Freestone said.

'Will the dramatic society survive?'

'Unlikely. I intend to leave anyway.'

'Because of Mason?'

'That's the catalyst, but the whole affair has brought out the worst in the people. Before, the members would meet, enjoy the moment, and then we'd go our separate ways, but now there is suspicion and doubt. There are unpleasant truths about all of us that we would prefer not to confront.'

'Such as?' Tremayne asked as he drank his beer.

'That two of us are murderers seems as good as any.'

'You realise that this land deal we're investigating is a strong motive.'

'I'll give you my word that I was not involved,' Freestone said.

'I'll accept your word, but we've got professionals checking it out.'

'Sure, I've made certain that the roads near where I live are in good condition, the local park is well looked after, but I've not taken money. My conscience is clear on this one.'

'The re-enactment,' Tremayne said, changing the subject.

'It's all arranged. Everyone will be there. How do you want to do this? And remember, we have no Julius Caesar.'

'Can you arrange a stand-in?'

'It's possible, but if we can't, you'll have to take part.'

'We need the full production. I can't learn the lines, and besides, I can't act.'

'Fine. I'll find someone.'

'If anyone feels like chickening out, let me know, and I'll organise a police car to pick them up.'

'And for the daggers? The ones up at Old Sarum are with you as evidence.'

'That's where they'll stay.'

'Fine. I'll organise some more. You can check them before we start.'

The two men ordered another pint. It was still early in the afternoon, and Tremayne knew he'd be working for a few more hours yet, at least until nine or ten in the evening. By that time, he'd arrive home, a quick brush of his teeth, or maybe not, before he collapsed into his bed. He thought about his ex-wife as he ate his meal and drank his beer. He remembered when they had first met, how he had woken up next to her the following morning, not remembering if they had made love, the months they had spent together before they had married, the drifting apart over the next few years, as he became a detective inspector.

The final straw had been when he came home in the early hours of the morning to find her sitting on the corner of the bed, dressed, two suitcases in the hallway downstairs.

'Sorry, Keith. I want a normal life, children, a dog in the garden.'

Tremayne remembered that day vividly. It wasn't as if the love between the two had waned; it was his devotion to his police work that had come between them. He could have said there and then that she was more important than his career, but he hadn't, couldn't, and then she was gone.

For over twenty-five years they had not spoken apart from the occasional phone call for the first couple of years after she had walked out, but she had met someone else, and then nothing.

He had contacted her after their previous case, and found she was widowed with two adult children. Their first meeting after so many years had been awkward and it had not been successful, but now there was a weekend away, and he was hopeful of a reconciliation. He realised that would impact on his policing. He knew he may have to make a decision: the ex-wife he still felt strongly about, but not sure if it was love, as that seemed more for Yarwood's age group.

There had been a few women over the years, but they had only been dalliances, no more than a passing attraction. One had moved in, wanted to change him, moved out within two months after realising that the man was an immovable object and it was either her or him. Apart from that, there had been very little love in his life. He regretted that as he sat with Freestone, a man who had been married to the same woman for nearly forty years, a man he may have to charge with murder within the next week.

He hoped it wasn't the accountant that he regarded as a friend. If it were, Tremayne would do his duty, he knew that.

'Who do you suspect?' Freestone asked.

'You've got a motive if we find anything underhanded,' Tremayne said. Peter Freestone was an intelligent man, so there was no point in telling him otherwise.

'Apart from me?'

'Who would you suspect?' Tremayne asked. 'Who do you think would have a violent streak? Who would have a reason to want the man dead?'

'Have you checked Mason's records?'

'Not in detail. The man was methodical, we know that. We've found no illegal dealings, nothing untoward.'

'He was tough as a solicitor. He must have ruffled a few feathers, put a few noses out of joint.'

'Enough to kill for?'

'Check with Len Dowling's brother.'

'Do you know anything?'

'Have you met Chris Dowling?'

'Yes. I met him with Sergeant Yarwood.'

'Aggressive?'

'He wanted to be.'

'I like Len,' Freestone said. 'Not his brother.'

'Any reason?'

'I don't trust him. He's too smart for me.'

'Any dirt on him?'

'Nothing specific.'

'Fiona Dowling?'

'My daughter went to school with Cheryl Milledge and Fiona Dowling. They used to come over to the house at weekends.'

'And?'

'Fiona was pretty, Cheryl was not. My daughter was friendly with them for a couple of years, and then they stopped coming.'

'Any reason why?'

'Nothing special. It's not the sort of conversation you have with your children. I was aware that Cheryl had changed, as had Fiona. Our daughter, thankfully, got through her adolescence without too much trouble. She came home a few times drunk, no doubt experimented with the boys, but not too much.'

'Your daughter told you that?'

'She'd speak to her mother, who'd tell me, not that I wanted to hear that our daughter was not the vestal virgin, no father wants to hear that.'

'What else can you tell me about Cheryl and Fiona?'

'Only titbits from our daughter. Cheryl started sleeping around, an unwanted pregnancy at one stage.'

'What happened to the child?'

'I've no idea. She may have aborted it or had the child adopted. I don't know the answer. I certainly didn't ask questions.'

'Fiona Dowling?'

'I used to see her around with Len Dowling. They were both no more than children then, and I was friends with Dowling's father.'

'Where is he now?'

'He went overseas, chasing the sun. I've lost contact with him.'

'What did the father say about Len and Fiona?'

'He was very fond of her, saw her as a good influence.'

'Is she?' Tremayne asked.

'She can be bossy, always wanting the lead female role. There's only two in *Julius Caesar*: Calpurnia, Caesar's wife and Portia, Brutus's wife.'

'Does she justify the lead role?'

'Most times, but Cheryl doesn't see it that way. To be honest, Cheryl is keen, but she's heavy on her feet. Calpurnia is assumed to be attractive, vivacious, not that anyone knows for sure.'

'Why do you mean?'

'We always assume that successful and powerful men have beautiful wives, that's all. Calpurnia could have been ugly for all we know, but she lived two thousand years ago.'

'Dennison qualifies on the successful and the beautiful wife.'

'The lovely Samantha.'

'Sarcasm or a genuine reflection of the woman?'

'Sarcasm, I suppose. She's a knockout, no doubt keeps Dennison happy, but she's not my type.'

'Why do you say that?'

'She's high-maintenance.'

'A driven woman?'

'Fiona is. Samantha Dennison would be as well. Fiona portrays herself as a socialite, into charitable causes, always there supporting her husband. Samantha makes no pretence of what she is.'

'Are you saying that Fiona is tarred with the same brush.'

'As I said, a driven woman.'

'Capable of murder?'

'How would I know? It may be something you're used to, Tremayne, but the majority of us live our lives oblivious to the harsh realities. I've seen death, who hasn't at our age, but I've not experienced murder before. All I've said is that Fiona and Samantha are determined.'

'And Cheryl Milledge?'

'She's latched on to Gary Barker. That man's not going far.'

As far as a profitable garden centre on the outskirts of Salisbury, Tremayne thought but did not mention it to Freestone.

***

Tremayne and Clare met back in the office. It was dark outside, and it was close to eight in the evening. Tremayne wanted an early finish, Clare did not. In the office and during the day, she was fine, but the nights still remained difficult. It was hard not to think of Harry.

She had to agree that Trevor Winston and his team had done a great job on her hair, but who was it for? Harry would have complimented her on how lovely she looked; Tremayne wouldn't even notice. Still, she was better in Salisbury, in that the tears were slowly drying up. Back with her parents, her father had wanted to distract her from her recollection of Harry; her mother had told her to get out into the dating market again, find a good man, a good Christian, an every Sunday at the church man. The only every Sunday at the church man she knew in the current case had been Gordon Mason, a misogynist bigot. No thanks, she thought.

If another man came into her life – and she felt almost guilty that she even considered it, so soon after Harry's death – she wouldn't care what he was as long as he was kind to her. Harry had been, but love was not about choosing the perfect mate based on a set of criteria. Samantha Dennison had done

119

that, and hers was a pretend happiness. Fiona Dowling had evaluated her mate and then moulded him into what she wanted. No, Clare knew it would be love, the only criterion that mattered, and she would not try to change the man.

She knew it served no purpose to think of the past when the present was all around her, and when there was an active murder case about to be burst open. The motives, the skeletons, the rumours, were all coming together.

'Yarwood, what do we have?' Tremayne said. He had seen his sergeant drifting off into memory land. He had given her a few minutes while he collected his own thoughts.

'We've not found any wrongdoing at the council offices so far. Cheryl Milledge was there, helping us.'

'She's the one who could have made the changes, you do realise that?'

'She's an administrator. She may have been involved, but I'm not so sure.'

'Why?'

'If the documents were altered, it would need someone to prepare them, the building inspector to see them, and then someone to register the change.'

'And?'

'I think we may be chasing a red herring here.'

'I still don't trust Len Dowling, nor his brother,' Tremayne said.

'Neither do I. If I'm buying a property in Salisbury, I know where I'm not going.'

'If you can find an agent who's any better, let me know.'

'You've met Peter Freestone,' Clare said. 'What did he have to say?'

'He knew Fiona Dowling and Cheryl Milledge as schoolgirls.'

'Any observations?'

'Fiona, he reckoned, is driven; Cheryl rolls with the punches.'

'Cheryl's a smart woman, don't underestimate her.'

'Capable of murder?'

120

'I've no idea. She's smart, devoted to Gary Barker from what I could make out.'

'Her records at the council?'

'Considering the condition of that awful bedsit they share, her files were correctly labelled, and her work area was spotless.'

If we're discounting the land deal, then what is the motive?'

'It has to be blackmail.'

'There's Fiona Dowling's affair. Did the man have some dirt on Dennison or his wife? He'd acted inappropriately towards Cheryl Milledge.'

'Dennison's wife may have a history. According to her, she had a background.'

'Background of what? By the way, your hair looks nice.'

'I didn't think you'd noticed.'

'I'm not good with compliments.'

'Thanks, it's appreciated.'

'Can we get back to the case instead of going on about your hair?'

Clare could see that the man was embarrassed at showing kindness. She liked him even more for his saying the right thing.

Tremayne leant back on his chair; Clare rested her back against the office wall. The day had been long; both were tired.

'Samantha Dennison said that I should find myself a rich man,' Clare said.

'That's not your style.'

'I know that, but if Dennison's wealth was threatened, he knows that Samantha would be off very quickly.'

'Are you suggesting that Mason could have impacted Dennison's wealth?'

'It's possible, although I'm not sure how. Gordon Mason was financially comfortable, lived frugally. Why would he care about Dennison?'

'He had insulted Samantha, had an altercation with Dennison. Maybe Mason bore a grudge.'

'That's possible, but how could he have an impact on Dennison?'

'Check it out,' Tremayne said. 'Dennison's playing the financial markets, no doubt using offshore bank accounts to hide his money from the tax man. There's also the possibility of insider trading. That's a criminal offence, time in jail. That's a motive, even better than a fraudulent land deal.'

'I'll look into it tomorrow,' Clare said.

'I'm off home, fancy a pint on the way?'

'I'll drink orange juice.'

'Yarwood, there's no hope for you. A police officer who can't drink a pint.'

'I had a glass of champagne with Samantha Dennison.'

'You don't want my definition of champagne, do you?'

'Not tonight I don't.'

Chapter 15

Bill Ford seemed to be the only one of the dramatic society who had no skeletons, no axe to grind. According to Freestone, the man attended rehearsals and the performances, put in a solid effort, and would have a drink afterwards at a local pub, but apart from that he did not socialise, abuse the women, threaten the men.

Freestone acknowledged that he and his wife would take the man out for the occasional meal, more out of sorrow for him after the death of his wife. But even then, he couldn't say that he knew Bill Ford in that he said little about his life.

Years of experience had told Tremayne that no one is without some misdemeanours, something they regretted, a wrong turn in life. He knew that he needed to find out, see if the man had an Achilles heel that would turn him from passive to active, something that could be construed as a motive.

It was cold in the back room of the funeral home where Ford was preparing an old man for his funeral, the coffin open for his nearest and dearest to say their fond farewells. Tremayne knew the deceased, having run him in on a couple of occasions for grievous bodily harm. He thought that he'd have no one crying over him, but according to Ford, the man's family were paying for the full treatment.

'Mr Ford,' Tremayne said, oblivious to the man continuing to work. Clare thought it disrespectful, but said nothing. 'We've interviewed everyone so far in depth apart from you.'

'I've spoken to you on a couple of occasions.'

'That we understand, but so far we know very little about you.'

'What's to tell? I do my job, go home, go to London on a regular basis.'

'Our problem still remains with a motive.'

'Mason wasn't the easiest man to get along with.'

'But murder?'

'Who knows what goes through the minds of people.'

'Which people, anyone in particular?' Tremayne asked.

Bill Ford continued to prepare the dead man. 'Sorry, but I'm working to a schedule here. The relatives will be here within the next two hours.'

Tremayne knew that some of those coming would not be pleased to see him. They were a family of villains, but apparently with money, judging by the meticulous care that the funeral director was taking with the body.

'You mentioned people. Anyone in mind?'

'I joined the dramatic society to get out of the house after my wife died. I didn't join to pry into anyone else's business.'

'But you're an astute man, you must have seen something.'

'The one thing about my regular friends is that they say very little, they mind their own business, and they don't become involved,' Ford said, nodding his head in the direction of the dead man.

'We're very much alive, we're police officers, and we do become involved. It's unfortunate, but I must continue to probe. Gordon Mason died for a reason, a reason that still remains unclear.'

'The man wasn't popular.'

'It's not a reason for murder. Did you like him, Mr Ford?'

'I neither like nor dislike anyone. I'm friendly with Peter Freestone and his wife. Gordon Mason was a fellow actor. We'd meet with the group, discuss the script, assign the roles, practise our lines. Apart from that, I rarely spoke to the man.'

Tremayne could see that the conversation was going nowhere. He looked over at Clare. She knew that he wanted her to become involved.

'Mr Ford, we are aware of reasons for your fellow actors to dislike Gordon Mason, but none seems strong enough to want him dead,' Clare said.

''Look at this man,' Ford said, pointing to the dead man. 'He was loved.'

'What's your point?'

'I've met his family, I know some of his past, yet he was loved. Gordon Mason was not loved, certainly by nobody that I knew of. Why do you think that is?'

'I've no idea. What do you think?'

'I don't think. It's just strange that a person can have a life devoid of any affection, that's all.'

'It's hardly a reason for murder. Tell us about your fellow actors.'

'As long as I don't miss my deadline. My client isn't concerned as to time, but his family is.'

'Okay, brief, single sentence answers.'

'Fire away.'

'Peter Freestone?'

'Decent and honest.'

'Phillip Dennison?'

'Wealthy, likes to show it off, attractive wife.'

'Any more to say about Samantha Dennison?'

'No. It's not my concern that she's a lot younger than her husband. That's between her and him.'

'Jimmy Francombe?'

'Young, keen, always cheerful.'

'Geoff Pearson?'

'Ambitious man. The women like him.'

'Anyone in particular?'

'I don't become involved.'

'It's a murder enquiry, Mr Ford,' Tremayne said. 'If you know anything, it's your civic responsibility to tell us.'

'Fiona Dowling liked him.'

'Anything more?'

'Mason suspected something.'

'I thought you didn't speak to him.'

'Once or twice he'd want to talk. He assumed I was a religious man, the same as him.'

'Are you?'

'I believe, but that's all. I've not seen anything to make me a fervent believer like Mason. My religion is private, moderate, and above all else non-critical. If Pearson and Dowling's wife were involved, it's between them and her husband. Mason didn't see it that way.'

'How did he see it?'

'He saw it as a sin against the Lord.'

'Did he tell Len Dowling?'

'He didn't like him.'

'But did he tell him?'

'You'll need to ask Len Dowling.'

Clare pressed on, aware that the man was non-committal with all his answers. It appeared to her that was how the man lived his life: a cold fish who neither loved nor hated, expressed anger or joy. Clare assumed it was as a result of spending too much time with the dead, being soulful and understanding with the relatives. Whatever it was, she didn't like it. To her, life was for the living, not standing for hours in a windowless room with only a corpse for company. She wanted out of that foreboding place and some fresh air.

'Gary Barker?'

'Easy-going, drinks more than he should.'

'I thought you weren't concerned about other people.'

'Drink himself under a table as far as I'm concerned, but he drinks and drives, that's all. One day, he'll have an accident, and then it'll be him in here or someone he hit.'

'Cheryl Barker?'

'Strong-willed. Keeps Gary under control.'

'Capable of losing her temper, capable of hate?'

'I'm not sure about hate, but she has a temper.'

'Any examples?'

'Her and Fiona Dowling don't get on.'

'They went to school together.'

'I know that.'

'How?'

'I took Fiona out once or twice before she met Len.'

'You're a few years older?'

'Only five or six.'

'It's eight actually.'

'Anyway, we went out together.'

'And what happened?'

'We were in our teens, or at least she was. I was in my early twenties. It was fun for a while.'

It was the first time that Ford had even referred to the possibility of fun. His countenance all the times they had encountered the funeral director rarely showed emotion and never a smile.

'Does Len Dowling know this?'

'I've never told him, and I doubt if Fiona has.'

'Why's that?'

'Dowling knows of his wife's wild behaviour in her teens. I doubt if she wanted to elaborate on it. She'd rather forget, no doubt.'

'But you're a remembrance.'

'I was just one of many. I don't intend to denigrate Fiona. I've some fond memories, one of the few times in my life when I felt free.'

'You don't feel free now?'

'What do you think?'

'I couldn't do what you do,' Clare said.

'Family tradition. Someone had to carry on with the business.'

'Coming back to Fiona. Did Cheryl know about you two?'

'There was one night when she came out with us.'

'And what happened?'

'The three of us ended up in my bed,' Ford said.

Tremayne looked up in shock, Clare felt like sitting down. The man with no apparent vices, no joy, had a past.

'Why have you told us?' Clare asked.

'I don't know. Maybe I just wanted to relive another time when I wasn't a funeral director.'

'Did Gordon Mason know about this?'

'I may have told him.'

'But why?'

'I don't know. Sometimes I get melancholy, feel like standing up on the roof and shouting.'

'You've spent too long in here with these bodies,' Tremayne said.

'It's a family tradition. The Fords have been funeral directors in Salisbury for the last one hundred and ten years.'

'You need to get out of here more often,' Tremayne said.

'I can't end the tradition.'

Tremayne and Clare left the man to his work. As they left the building, Tremayne could see some villains coming their way. He took hold of Yarwood's arm and steered her into a café nearby.

'What do you reckon?' Tremayne asked.

'The man has a macabre personality. Too long with those bodies has affected him.'

'Capable of murder?'

'Capable of anything. The only spark in him was when he spoke about Fiona and Cheryl.'

'That came as a shock.'

'It's a motive, especially if Mason knew. Fiona's not his murderer, though.'

'She wouldn't want it bandied around that she had indulged in a threesome. Her social set would accept that she had been wild in her youth, but a threesome has connotations of perversion. She would do anything to protect that information.'

'What about Cheryl?'

'Would she care what people think of her? Her past is an open book.'

***

Tremayne and Clare returned to Bemerton Road Police Station. On Tremayne's desk, an official letter marked private and confidential.

'Important, guv?' Clare asked. She had seen Tremayne looking at it with contempt.

'It's Moulton again, trying to intimidate me into retiring.'

'He can't do that.'

'He can intimidate, keep up the heat in the hope that I'll cave in.'

'Will you?'

'What do you reckon, Yarwood?'

'Can he force you?'

'No.'

'Then why ask me? Just ignore him. We've got a murder enquiry to deal with.'

'Yarwood, you're becoming pushy.'

'I've had a good teacher.'

'I suppose so,' Tremayne replied, a smile on his face.

'Bill Ford, what do you reckon?' Clare asked.

'How did he become like that?'

'Life takes turns you least expect. It's certainly had some effect on him, and he'd be inured to the sight of death.'

'A potential murderer?'

'They all are.'

'As I told you, Yarwood, everyone has skeletons in the cupboard. Everyone is capable of causing harm to another if their life or their families are threatened.'

Tremayne looked around his office, realised that he had paperwork to do, but not today. Yarwood, he could see, was all the better for being busy. The man wanted out of the office and soon.

As the two prepared to leave a familiar if not welcome face appeared at the door. 'A moment of your time, Detective Inspector.'

Clare could see the look on her senior's face, the look of determination on Superintendent Moulton's.

'What can I do for you?' Tremayne asked. Clare thought Tremayne was brusque in his reply.

'You've seen my letter?'

'It's not the first one.'

'And not the last, either.'

'I thought we'd resolved this.'

'The Police Federation have, I realise that, but there's a directive from senior management to bring in fresh blood,'

Moulton said. Tremayne knew that the directive was a recommendation, not an order. He had contacts in other police stations within the region that were going through the same exercise. Some of his contemporaries had accepted, some hadn't.

'It's a generous package,' Moulton said.

'I never said it wasn't, but I'm comfortable. The house is paid off, I've no debts.'

'Put your feet up, enjoy yourself.'

Clare, who should not have been listening, but was only eight feet away at her desk, realised that Moulton did not understand. The man was career-driven, Tremayne was results-driven, and he was enjoying himself. She had to admit that she was, as well. She hoped the feeling of a job well done, the satisfaction of a result, would not leave her. If it did, she knew that she may as well be back at her parents' hotel as manager.

She had considered it for a time while she was consumed with grief, but it had not helped. There were too many times to reflect back to Harry, too many hours between the guests leaving and their replacements arriving. She knew that with Tremayne and a murder enquiry it was full on from morning to night, and then exhaustion once she made it back to her cottage. The cats that Harry had had an issue with would be waiting for her, a warm bed that she would share with them. She had heard the rustling of the branches, their scraping against the roof, an owl hooting in the distance, even deer in the field behind, but she had felt no fear.

In fact, the place was coming up for sale. She needed Tremayne and his Homicide department, the security of the police force, for the finance. Her parents, she knew, would have lent her the money, but she did not want their input; it would come with conditions, and her mother would be down at the cottage advising on what colour to paint the walls, the style of furniture, the need to find another man.

Tremayne, the cantankerous detective inspector, would never offer advice, would always be there for her. Clare realised that she appreciated his company more than that of her parents.

She thought it was wrong somehow, but she could not alter the facts.

'Yarwood, are you ready or are you going to sit there all day?'

'Superintendent Moulton?'

'He'll leave us alone. The man's a pain, always worrying about his key performance indicators, whatever they are.'

'You don't know?'

'I know what they are. I just don't understand the relevance. He talks about lowering the average age of the people in the station, reducing expenditure, and only hiring degree-educated people.'

'They're important. Maybe not the age issue.'

'The man means well, I suppose, and we always need people in Administration.'

'Administration? He's a police officer.'

'Administration. He doesn't understand villains. Probably never met one.'

'He was out on the street once,' Clare said.

'If he was, he's forgotten what it was like. He wanted to give me a lecture on how to conduct a murder investigation. The man's probably never seen a murder victim.'

'I'm sure he has, guv.'

'Yarwood, let me have my two minutes. The man irritates me, and I've got to call him sir. I know what I'd call him if I had half a chance.'

'He can't make you retire, correct?'

'Not for another couple of years.'

'Then why worry about him?'

'You're right, Yarwood. What's next? Who haven't we interviewed?'

'We've interviewed everyone. They've all got reasons to not like Mason, but none has admitted to killing him.'

'Do they ever?'

'The re-enactment's this weekend.'

'We'll go and see Freestone, check that it's all organised.'

Chapter 16

Phillip Dennison had gone short on the exchange rate between the American dollar and the English pound when he should have gone long. Most days he read it right, but it had been three in a row now, and he was worried. His wife was continuing to spend as if there was no tomorrow, which in her case, he thought may be possible.

He didn't know why she was that way. When they had met, she had been beautiful and genuinely desirable, but since he had joined the dramatic society as a way of reducing his stress, she had become difficult, unable to listen to criticism, unwilling to curb her spending when the finances were precarious. He knew it could not continue. He needed out.

Dennison made a phone call.

'What can I do for you?' Chris Dowling asked on picking up his phone.

'We need to meet.'

'My office, forty-five minutes.'

Dennison left his laptop on, the negatives in his account visible on the screen. He left the house and drove to Salisbury. The Aston Martin was with his wife; he took a BMW. It was her car really and when he had bought it for her, she had been delighted, but now it was a never-ending cycle of increased spending on cars and holidays and clothes that remained in the bags that she had brought them home in. His situation was desperate; Chris Dowling was his way out.

He found Dowling in his office. He'd seen the Aston Martin parked next to one of the most expensive shops in the city on his way there. He remembered her in that office when they had first met. How he had lusted after her. He had seen the young men with their eyes peering at her, taking every opportunity to be close to her, but it had been him with his wealth who had won her.

She wasn't the first that had succumbed, she wouldn't be the last, although the next time he'd be more careful. Or maybe he wouldn't, he knew that. When the market was running, and he was on a winning streak, the money would flow in. He needed an outlet. The dramatic society had provided it for the last couple of years; before that, it had been expensive cars and expensive women. Now, one woman was causing him aggravation. That day, as he entered Chris Dowling's office, he was down over one hundred thousand pounds, and that was likely to increase by at least another two thousand by the time his wife had finished exercising her gold credit card.

'Look, Dowling, I'm desperate. The woman's bleeding me dry.'

'I said at the time that she was going to cause you trouble.'

'I know. I didn't listen.'

'I told you to put an agreement in place, but what did you do?'

'I loved her.'

'Dennison, you may be a hotshot money man, but you're clueless with women. It's one thing to seduce women like Samantha, it's another to keep them. What do you think she finds attractive in you: your good looks, your good manners?'

'I know. Don't lecture.'

'You can divorce her, but she'll take half your assets.'

'She's welcome to them today.'

'That bad?'

'Tomorrow I'll make it up.'

'No doubt you will, but Samantha's not going away. As long as you indulge her, she'll stay.'

'I'll talk to her tonight. Tell her what's happening,' Dennison said.

'She'll not be responsive to your charms afterwards.'

'She hasn't been for some time.'

'Women like her need a man in their bed. Any suspicions?'

'None that I know of. Do you believe that's possible?'

'We've known each other for a long time, what do you think?'

'With who?'

'How the hell would I know? She's your wife, you ask her. And take the keys of the Aston Martin. You don't want her fancy man driving it, do you?'

***

'It's all arranged,' Peter Freestone said. This time Clare had asked him not to smoke his pipe.

'A stand-in for Caesar?' Tremayne asked.

'I've got someone.'

'Another actor?'

'He doesn't often come, but he will as a special favour to me.'

'He owes you one?'

'I've offered to help him out with a business plan. It's costing me to help you.'

'You're still a suspect,' Tremayne said.

'Hopefully, you'll deduce who is the guilty party at the re-enactment. It's not much fun sitting in a pub with a man who thinks you might be a murderer.'

'It's not much fun for me either,' Tremayne said. 'At least you'll drink a beer. Yarwood's on orange juice, champagne even.'

'Just the once,' Clare said.

'We've drawn a blank on your rezoning. It appears that it was above board.'

'Len Dowling took the risk, reaped the reward,' Freestone said.

'He's still a suspect.'

'Who isn't?'

'Until this is wrapped up, everyone is. Do you deal with Dennison's tax returns?'

'I have in the past, not recently.'

'Anything unusual?'

'The man understands his tax liabilities, structures his dealings accordingly.'

'Any suggestion of tax avoidance?'

'If there were, I'd be required to notify the authorities.'

'Would you?'

'Don't use Dennison as a way of getting at me again. I've been honest with you.'

'You've seen where he lives, the car his wife drives. Do his tax returns reflect his income?'

'I prepare his tax returns based on the information received from him.'

'That's not what I asked.'

'I know that. I would have prepared Dennison's tax returns based on the information received. He, as with any other client, will sign that they are declaring the truth. I will then sign that I've prepared the return based on the client's input. Legally, I've acted in accordance with the law.'

'You've still not answered my question,' Tremayne said.

'I have.'

***

The last person that was expected at the re-enactment was Samantha Dennison, but there she was, sitting in the front row. The cast were all there, although Fiona Dowling had been late arriving, and Len Dowling was complaining about a potential lost sale.

Phillip Dennison did not appear to be in a good mood, casting glances at his wife, for once dressed sensibly. Nobody seemed to be in the best of humour, apart from Gary Barker and Cheryl Milledge, both of whom had come in costume.

Tremayne took centre stage at the old fort. 'Ladies and gentlemen, thanks for coming tonight. I've asked Jim Hughes, our crime scene examiner, to be present. It's not usual for him to

135

attend a re-enactment. I've asked him as a special favour as we still have the issue of how Gordon Mason died.'

'I thought that was clear,' Bill Ford said.

'You're correct in that we know that he died from two stab wounds to the heart, as well as three others. Four of the five would have ultimately been fatal. The question is, how did those who committed the murder know which dagger would kill him, and how were the fake daggers swapped?'

'Was every dagger we carried on that stage modified?' Geoff Pearson asked. Clare noticed that he was standing at some distance from Fiona Dowling, his latest girlfriend sitting to one side of Samantha Dennison.

'Two were.'

'And you don't know who held those two?' Cheryl Milledge asked.

'No. We're assuming that whoever had the lethal daggers knew. Jim is certain that a retractable dagger punching the man's body and one that entered would have distinctly different feels. There is some conjecture on this, as in the scene, frenetic as it was, an adrenaline rush may have confused those taking part. Regardless, we need to see if that was the case. There is also the additional factor of how the daggers were swapped. Peter Freestone brought the fakes here, two of you have testified that they were indeed plastic bladed and harmless. That means the swap occurred here.'

'Someone would have seen,' Fiona Dowling said.

'Not necessarily. It was dark.'

'It can't be Cheryl or me.'

'We know there were two daggers, which would suggest two men,' Tremayne said. 'Can we be certain that Mason was not stabbed off the stage? It would not have to be a man then. We have, more than likely, two murderers here tonight, possibly three, maybe only one. We need to know how many and who.'

'It makes no sense,' Gary Barker said. 'The man was not liked, but three people. What's the motive?'

'There are motives, but none seem sufficient for murder, and if they were, how do those responsible expect to maintain

their innocence. We will find out who did it and they will be
arrested. I've also arranged for two police cars, five uniforms to
be present.'

'That's intimidation,' Dennison said.

'It's policing. Someone here is a murderer. They can either
admit to their guilt now, save us all a cold night up here, or we'll
carry on. Any takers?'

Clare looked around to see innocent looks on all the
faces. Samantha Dennison, not present on the night of Mason's
murder, scowled. Clare could see that the situation between her
and her husband was not good. She walked over to her.
'Samantha, I'm surprised to see you here,' Clare said.

'Phillip's threatened me.'

'How?'

'He's had his solicitor on to me.'

'Why?'

'He's a bastard, that's why. Phillip wants to clip my wings,
take the Aston Martin away from me.'

'You do spend a lot.'

'He knew the deal.'

'Is he trading up?'

'The younger model? No. I think he's lost the edge. He
can't afford me.'

'You'll take off?'

'Once I've secured my share of the deal.'

'And what's that?'

'Half the assets.'

'For four years of marriage?'

'Phillip did say he'd see me right when the time came.'

'In writing?'

'He's pleading poverty.'

'Maybe he is.'

'Not him. He's stashing it somewhere, and he's got
someone making sure I can't get my hands on it.'

'Any idea who?'

'He's using Chris Dowling as his solicitor.'

'You know the man?'

'We've met.'

Clare left the woman and went back over to where Tremayne and Freestone were setting up the re-enactment. 'She's a bitter woman,' Clare said to Tremayne.

'You've seen Phillip Dennison. He's not in the best of humour either.'

Jim Hughes was with Freestone, discussing the daggers. 'These are the ones I've purchased for tonight,' Freestone said. Hughes ran his fingers over the blades, checked the retracting mechanism. He declared them harmless.

***

Tremayne and Clare had focussed on the assassination scene, not the entire production, up to now. The idea that three people could have been involved seemed illogical. And even if it was three, the question remained as to why kill the man on a stage in front of a group of people. If Mason had deserved to die, at least in the minds of the murderers, then why at Old Sarum? The man, it was known, lived in a depressingly drab house not far from Salisbury. Tremayne and Clare had been out there after his death, found nothing of interest, just an unkempt garden, a house that smelt of disinfectant, and not much else, not even a television. There was a library, complete with books, but most were legal or thrillers, neither of which interested Tremayne.

Peter Freestone, directing as well as playing the part of Brutus, was a busy man. The scene where Mason was killed was some way into the production. Firstly, there were three scenes in Act 1, four scenes in Act 2, not that most people knew the full play, only Mark Antony's speech to the crowd inciting them against the conspirators, and little else.

Friends, Romans and countrymen, lend me your ears,
I come to bury Caesar, not to praise him…

What concerned Tremayne was how the daggers had been changed and when, and what could have occurred before

138

the assassination. The crowd scenes involved some of Jimmy Francombe's school friends. Clare had spoken to them, received the Francombe chat-up lines, been asked about the hot date.

She had brushed them off with a smile, realising that they were just the same as Jimmy: polite, full of testosterone, and desperate to show their friends that they were better than them.

Act 1, Scene 1, and Bill Ford and Gary Barker were on stage, playing the parts of Flavius and Marullus respectively. Two of Jimmy's friends were playing the two commoners, one a carpenter, the other a cobbler. Clare sat out the front with Samantha Dennison. Tremayne was around the back. The problem with the re-enactment, Tremayne could see, was that the people taking part were not taking it seriously; there was no sense of urgency. The first act had concluded and Act 1, Scene 2 should have commenced promptly, but it was five minutes, and no one was on the stage. It was the first scene for Caesar, as well as for Casca, Calpurnia, Mark Antony, the soothsayer, Brutus, Cassius, and Trebonius. Caesar was being played by William Bradshaw, an actor who had come down from Swindon, a city about forty miles north of Salisbury. As Freestone had said, the man was familiar with the part, having played it in another production. Tremayne knew that the man was not involved, as he had not been present on the night of Mason's death.

The soothsayer, eight lines in total, a minor part, although with the immortal line *Beware the ides of March,* was played by Robert Hemsworth, a local schoolteacher. Freestone had told Tremayne earlier that the man rarely attended their meetings, never came to the pub, and was not friendly. He was, however, dependable, punctual, and a decent actor. Tremayne had discounted him from being involved. He knew that whoever had swapped the daggers had to have a tie-in with the conspirators. Trebonius, one of the conspirators, played by Hemsworth's brother, James, had not been present at the stabbing, as his part required that he had to take Mark Antony out of the Senate when Caesar was assassinated.

Ten minutes later, instead of one, the actors filed onto the stage for Act 1, Scene 2. Trevor Winston was in costume, as was Jimmy Francombe; the others were not.

Clare looked at Samantha Dennison as her husband came onto the stage; she could see the contempt in the woman's face. 'What are you going to do, Samantha?'

'I've told you.'

'He's brought you tonight. He must care.'

'He wants to keep an eye on me.'

'Why?'

'In case I do something foolish.'

'Is that likely?'

'It's always possible.'

'What sort of thing?'

'Cut his clothes with a pair of scissors, run the edge of a coin down his Aston Martin.'

'That seems extreme.'

'Not for that bastard, it isn't. He's taken my credit cards.'

'Samantha, someone murdered Gordon Mason. If it's your husband, he could murder you.'

'Not him.'

'Are you certain? I don't want to be the one who has to identify you.'

'Do you think he could do something?'

'I don't know. I suggest you don't provoke him.'

'I already have.'

'How?'

'I told him I had a lover.'

'Is it true?'

'I told him it was Geoff Pearson.'

'Is it true?'

'If he had money it could be, but no.'

'And your husband's reaction?'

'He slapped me across the face, called me a shameless tart, no better than a common prostitute.'

'What did you do?'

'I came here tonight.'

140

'And Geoff Pearson?'
'Phillip will do nothing.'
'Are you sure?'
'I hope I am.'

Chapter 17

Act 1, Scene 3, and Len Dowling was playing the additional role of Cicero, the only scene in the play where the character appears. Dowling had used a wig to change his appearance on the night of the production. The parts of Casca, Cassius, and Cinna were again played by Trevor Winston, Geoff Pearson, and Gary Barker respectively. Cicero came on with Casca, said his lines and departed, and Cassius walked on.

Tremayne occupied himself around the back looking for an opportunity to change the daggers, realising that the two lethal weapons could have been hidden under the Roman robes the actors wore. He also realised that all he was going to get that night was cold and wet. It had started to drizzle, and those who had been standing outside or sitting on the grass had moved to somewhere under cover. Tremayne looked for Yarwood; he could see her talking to Samantha Dennison. He did not want to disturb her.

'Do you want to carry on?' Freestone asked. 'They're starting to complain about the weather.'

'Would you have cancelled on the night because of a little rain?'

'No.'

'Then that's what we'll do. So far, I've not seen how the daggers were changed.'

'Don't ask me. I only put on the production, take a leading role on stage.'

The weather improved, the production continued: Act 2, Scenes 1 to 4 passed by. Tremayne focussed on the daggers, aiming to get an angle on how it was done, and on why the man was murdered during a production of Shakespeare's *Julius Caesar*, and for what reason.

The most crucial scene, at least for Tremayne, was Act 3, Scene 1: a crowd of people, Jimmy Francombe's friends, amongst them the soothsayer and Artemidorus.

Caesar speaks to the soothsayer: *The ides of March are come.*

The soothsayer responds: *Ay, Caesar; but not gone.*

Artemidorus, played by another friend of Jimmy Francombe, attempts to warn Caesar about those who plot against him.

Then Caesar's entry into the Senate, Metellus pleading for Caesar to end the banishment of his brother, the casting aside of his request.

The daggers plunging into Caesar: the first by Casca, and then the others, Cassius, Cinna, Metellus, Decius Brutus, Ligarius, and, finally, Brutus.

Tremayne could see it clearly. The two murderers on the stage had the daggers that had killed Mason hidden inside their robes. Whoever they were, they had brought them with them.

Tremayne went over to where Clare was sitting. 'I've seen enough,' he said.

Clare excused herself to Samantha Dennison and walked away with Tremayne. 'You know who did it?'

'I know how the daggers were brought in.'

'How?'

'The two who killed Mason had them hidden under their clothes when they came to Old Sarum, and after they changed into costume, they hid them under their robes. It's easy once you see it,' Tremayne said.

'No idea on who, though?'

'None. What's the deal with Dennison's wife?'

'He's clipped her wings.'

'Why?'

'According to her, he's taken away her credit cards, the key to the Aston Martin.'

'She'll not like that. She'll be off soon.'

'She wants her money first.'

'How much?'

'Half of everything that the husband has.'

'She'll be lucky. What security does she have?'

'Only his word. She may have genuinely loved him at first,' Clare said.

'And now?'

'I don't think there's much love left. He threatened her; she told him that Geoff Pearson was her lover.'

'Is he?'

'According to her, he's not.'

'If Dennison's a murderer, then Pearson's compromised.'

'We need to talk to Dennison,' Clare said. 'The man's threatened his wife, and now he believes she's cheating on him.'

Tremayne left Clare and went back to Peter Freestone. 'You can wrap it up. I've seen enough.'

'We were just about to go anyway. Did you get what you wanted?'

'I think so.'

'The murderer or murderers?'

'Not yet, but the pieces are coming together.'

'Don't ask for another re-enactment,' Freestone said.

'Why?'

'We're disbanding, too much has happened. It was fun, but now we don't feel comfortable in each other's company. Maybe after this is all over, but for now, we'll not meet, at least not as a dramatic society.'

'Sorry to hear that,' Tremayne said.

***

The body was found ninety minutes later. By that time, virtually everyone had gone, apart from Tremayne, Clare, and Peter Freestone. The first they knew that something was wrong was when Geoff Pearson's new girlfriend from Southampton came running over to them. 'I can't find Geoff,' she said.

Up till that time Clare had taken little notice of her, apart from saying hello to her when she arrived.

'We'd thought you'd gone.'

'We were leaving and then we decided to take a walk around outside, where the old cathedral was.'

'What happened?'

'We were fooling around, seeing who could get to the car first. I'm up ahead, Geoff's behind me, and then all of a sudden, nothing. I thought he was just playing a game. I went back, but I couldn't see him.'

'We'll find him,' Tremayne said.

Two uniforms, who had hoped for an early night, took out their torches and headed in the direction of the cathedral ruins. They came back within ten minutes. 'We've phoned for an ambulance,' one of them said.

'Is he hurt?' the girlfriend asked.

'I'm sorry.'

'Serious?' Clare asked.

'He's gone off the side of one of the ruined walls. There's a significant drop. He's landed heavily by the look of it.'

Tremayne and Clare, as well as the uniforms, the girlfriend, and Freestone, headed over to the area as fast as they could. It was dark, and the only torches were being held by the uniforms. 'He's down there,' one of the uniforms said.

Clare walked further along to some wooden steps. She descended, one of the uniforms with her, Geoff Pearson visible on the ground twenty feet in front of them. Clare approached the body, careful not to disturb the surrounding area, while the uniform shone the torch. She shouted up to Tremayne. 'We need Jim Hughes up here,' she said.

'Dead?'

'He's fallen heavily, broken his neck probably.'

The girlfriend collapsed into Tremayne's arms. He led her away.

Clare came back up the steps. The uniform shone his light at the area above where the body lay, the signs all too clear. 'It's murder. The man was pushed.'

She then phoned Hughes to confirm that the man's death was no longer suspicious as the signs of his being pushed were visible on the grass above where he fell.

Tremayne, once Clare had updated him, took control. The uniforms were establishing a crime scene, ensuring that no one else was in the area. Freestone confirmed that all the cars belonging to the dramatic society members had gone, except for Pearson's. The girlfriend sat in Clare's car, keeping warm with the heater on. Tremayne knew she would have to be interviewed and then taken home. Once again, as he'd expected, the one murder had become two; he was sure that Pearson would not be the last.

Clare came back from the crime scene, visibly upset.

'You need to detach yourself, Yarwood.'

'It's still sad.'

'Maybe it is, but we've got a job to do, and remember, he may have been one of the murderers.'

'Is that likely?'

'Why not? If he was, then the other one has dealt with him, destroying anyone who may have had a guilty conscience. What do you reckon?'

'Fiona Dowling, Phillip Dennison.'

'The spurned lover, the cheated husband. Anyone else?'

'Fiona Dowling won't be able to keep the affair secret from her husband.'

'Maybe he knew. He's a suspect as well. That's three. Any more?'

'It's enough to be going on with.'

'We're in for a long night.'

'Jim Hughes may be able to tell us if it was male or female.'

The crime scene team arrived at Old Sarum. They came equipped with a truck with a generator on the back. Within two hours, the site was ablaze with floodlights. A statement had been taken from the girlfriend, a blossoming romance in that she and Pearson had only been together for two weeks. Clare organised one of the police cars to take her home.

Tremayne was anxious for a definite suspect; Hughes was trying to do his job. 'Give me time, Tremayne,' Hughes said.

'Male or female?'

'The grass is damp underfoot. The man could have just slipped.'

'I don't believe it, neither does Yarwood.'

'And when did you two become experienced crime scene investigators?'

'It's murder, I know it is.'

'You may know it, but I need to prove it. They're not the same,' Hughes said.

Jim Hughes checked the man's body. It was clear that he had a broken neck, as Clare had ascertained, and that he had hit his head hard on the exposed wall of the cathedral as he fell, the blood visible in the grass beside the body. Hughes's team of investigators were up above, tracing the movements of three people: Geoff Pearson, his girlfriend, and the person responsible for pushing him over the wall. It was clear to Hughes that the fall, whereas a long drop, would not have automatically killed him. It would have caused broken bones and severe bruising, but the body would have been relaxed, not able to see where it was falling.

The verdict for him was either an unfortunate accident or attempted murder, as death was by no means certain. He knew Tremayne wanted clear proof of murder, but he was not going to get it.

'Okay, what is it?' Tremayne asked. He had moved away from the immediate area to smoke a cigarette, but now he was back.

'Yarwood was correct. The man's neck has been broken.'

'Male or female?'

'If you are referring to who he had an altercation with, then it's a female.'

'Are you certain?'

'We'll need to do further analysis, but the size of the shoe print is only small, the shape is feminine. Anyone you suspect?'

'A jilted lover.'

'Not the young girl that was here before?'

'She's not involved.'

'It's going to get nasty.'

'When hasn't it been. I'm afraid the Salisbury Amateur Dramatic Society is the same as everyone else, full of love and hatred.'

'A Shakespearean tragedy,' Hughes said.

'That's what it is,' Tremayne said. 'It's not over yet.'

***

Fiona Dowling arrived at Bemerton Road Police Station at two in the morning with her husband, Len. His brother, Chris, came five minutes later.

'You can't be in the interview, Mr Dowling,' Tremayne said to Len Dowling.

'Chris?'

'If he's Mrs Dowling's legal representative.'

'He will be.'

Tremayne commenced the interview, followed the procedure. At 2.38 a.m. the first question: 'Mrs Dowling, you are aware that Geoff Pearson has died at Old Sarum?'

'That was explained on the phone to me.'

'Do you wish to make a statement?'

'I was not involved. Why am I here?'

'Mrs Dowling, we have proof that Geoff Pearson was firmly pushed off the ruins of the old cathedral. We know from our crime scene team that a woman was close to him when he was pushed.'

'He was there with a young woman.'

'We've discounted her. And besides, she had no motive.'

'Neither do I.'

'Mrs Dowling, we know that you had a reason to hate the man,' Clare said.

'Does Chris need to be here?' Fiona Dowling asked.

'He is here at your request. I would suggest that he stays. The charge for Pearson's death will be murder, and at this time, all the evidence points towards you.'

'What proof do you have?' Chris Dowling said.

'We have a shoe print which will be subjected to further analysis. We also have a motive.'

'What motive?' Chris Dowling asked.

'Do I have to tell him?' Fiona Dowling asked Tremayne.

'We have sufficient proof to place a charge. It cannot be avoided.'

'It will destroy my marriage, my life.'

'I'm afraid that you should have considered that before.'

'Very well, but I did not push the man. It was an argument, that's all.'

'With his girlfriend nearby.'

'She wasn't his girlfriend. He had no right to be with her.'

'Why?'

'Because he was mine.'

'Fiona, what are you talking about?' Chris Dowling asked.

'We were lovers.'

'You and this man?'

'Why not? Your brother couldn't keep it up. I needed a man, a real man.'

Chris Dowling sat back, shocked by his sister-in-law's revelation.

'Mrs Dowling, you will be held in custody. Pending confirmation from the crime scene examiner, you will be charged with murder. Is there anything else that you wish to say in your defence?' Tremayne asked.

'Nothing. I was angry. I didn't know there was a drop. He belonged to me, not to that young girl.'

'It can be used in your defence,' Tremayne said. 'Are you able to assist in the murder of Gordon Mason? Was he blackmailing you over your affair? Did he know?'

'He knew. He wanted something in return to keep quiet.'

'What was that?'

'What do you think?'

'Sexual intercourse?' Clare said.

'With that awful man, no way. I've got my standards.'

'Instead of agreeing to his demand, you murdered the man.'

'I didn't kill him. You should have asked Geoff.'

'He denied it.'

'You believed him?'

'We had no reason to doubt him. He kept your secret.'

'He told Gordon Mason.'

'To our knowledge he did not. On the contrary, he was always discreet.'

'If he didn't, then who did?'

'We have no idea. Do you want to talk to your husband?'

'Not tonight. Chris can tell him.'

Chapter 18

Superintendent Moulton was pleased to have one murder solved; Tremayne was not. The killing of Gordon Mason remained predominant in his mind. The death of Geoff Pearson, caused by a possessive woman who had pushed him, was probably not premeditated. It seemed to Tremayne that pushing someone in anger in a grassy area, not knowing about the drop to one side, would not necessarily be construed as murder, and that manslaughter may well be the eventual verdict. Even so, to Fiona Dowling, a woman whose public persona was all important, her time in jail would be a death blow to her social aspirations.

'Yarwood, was Pearson involved in Gordon Mason's murder?' Tremayne asked.

'Fiona Dowling revealed that Mason knew about her affair. It could be a motive for Pearson.'

'I can see Pearson hitting the man, but not murder.'

'It's four in the morning, can we go home, guv?' Clare asked.

'I thought we were having fun.'

'Tomorrow, early, as much fun as you like. For now, I need to sleep.'

***

The news of Geoff Pearson's death and the subsequent arrest of Fiona Dowling sent shock waves throughout the dramatic society. Peter Freestone had wanted to disband the group, but now they had a common cause; the defence of Fiona, the shock and abhorrence at Pearson's death. Cheryl Milledge took it particularly badly, but then it was known that she was an emotional person, able to fall in love with ease, to fall out at the same rate, the reason that her love life had been so varied.

Cheryl was the first to react on hearing the news. She arrived at the police station at seven in the morning after a phone call from Peter Freestone, who had been kept updated as to the situation. 'I'd like to see Fiona Dowling,' Cheryl said to the police constable on duty in reception.

'Are you a relative?'

'I'm a friend.'

'I can't let you see her without the permission of Detective Inspector Tremayne.'

'Please ask. I'm sure he will allow me to see her. How is she?'

'I'm not sure I know. She was remanded last night; she's in the cells.'

Cheryl helped herself to coffee from the machine nearby and took a seat. Gary Barker was coming in later for moral support. After a ninety-minute wait, Clare walked in.

'Sergeant Yarwood, how is Fiona?' Cheryl stood upon her arrival to make sure that she was seen.

'As well as can be expected.'

'This has come as a complete shock.'

'You've known her longer than anyone else.'

The two women moved to Clare's desk in Homicide.

'Our story is known,' Cheryl said.

'We know that Gordon Mason knew about the affair.'

'Not from me.'

'Would Gary have said anything?'

'Gary wouldn't have wasted his time telling Gordon. He knows about my past, and he never mentions it. As far as Gary would be concerned, if Geoff was playing around with Fiona, then good luck to Geoff. Gary rolls with the punches; he doesn't take life too seriously.'

'The garden centre, he seemed keen on taking that over.'

'Only because he gets to play with the plants. He's not got a head for business.'

'Whereas you have?'

'It's a good business apart from his parents.'

'We're told that you don't get on with them.'

'Gary told you this?'

'Yes. Is it true?'

'They go to the same church that Mason did. If you think he was bad, you should meet Gary's parents.'

'He doesn't seem affected by them.'

'He left home in his teens, roamed around, got into trouble, nothing serious, before going back there.'

'That must have been hard.'

'It's best if you ask Gary.'

'You're here. I'm asking you.'

'Gary wasn't into drugs, not in a big way, but one day, after a severe reaction, he ends up on their doorstep. They take him in, get him detoxed. As long as he's got his plants, he's okay.'

'And his parents' fervent hatred of you?'

'They know about my past. They see me as a bad influence.'

'Have you been involved with drugs?'

'Not me, or at least not seriously. I smoked, still do. I tried marijuana when I was younger, snorted cocaine once or twice, but nothing more.'

'Alcohol?'

'More than I should. It doesn't control my life.'

'Who could have told Gordon Mason about Fiona Dowling and Geoff Pearson?'

'I'm not sure. I could see them looking at each other, not sure if her husband did, but then he was always a bit thick.'

'Salisbury's premier estate agent?'

'Fiona was the driving force, you must have known that. Sure, he can stand up, talk the talk, make you believe in Father Christmas, but he needed pointing in the general direction. Why do you think Fiona stayed with him?'

'I don't know,' Clare said. 'You tell me.'

'Fiona needs to control, and with Len, he was a prime candidate. He was someone she could mould.'

'Did she love her husband, does she?'

'She loved that she could mould him to what she wanted.'

'Bill Ford mentioned that you and he went out together in the past.'

'A long time ago, before he took over the funeral business from his father.'

'What can you tell me?'

'Is it relevant?'

'Probably not, but you're here. It's a question that begs an answer.'

'So did Fiona. What's he been telling you?'

'He said that you two had been wild, so had he.'

'He was fun back then. Now he's a boring man. It's hard to believe that they are one and the same.'

'Is that it?'

'If you want me to mention the threesome, then yes.'

'Fiona was possessive of Geoff Pearson. Have you seen that side of her personality before?'

'She likes to control, I've told you that.'

'Did she try to control you?'

'She always wanted to organise where we were going when we went out for the night. There's nothing strange with that. She was driven, I was not. We went our separate ways. She married Len, I moved from man to man.'

'Is she jealous of you now?'

'Fiona? I don't think so. She wouldn't fancy Gary.'

'Why not?'

'You've met Gary. He's not a person you can drive. He lets life pass him by, takes what it gives, asks no more.'

'Apart from the garden centre.'

'I gave him that idea.'

'Do you stay with him because of it?'

'Not a chance. It's there, I'm getting older. I want children, a home, a husband, someone to care for. Gary will always treat me well, and I've no intention of changing him. That's what Fiona likes doing, not me.'

'Would you like to see Mrs Dowling?'

'Yes, please.'

'I'll arrange it for you. You'd better get yourself another cup of coffee.'

***

Chris Dowling had the unenviable task of telling his brother, Len, what had transpired at the police interview, and the fact that his wife was being held in the cells at Bemerton Road Police Station.

'I didn't know,' Len said.

'Len, you can be stupid sometimes. Your wife is screwing Pearson, and you didn't suspect?'

'It's the truth. She's been a bit cold lately. I assumed it was because she was busy.'

'Do you believe that Fiona has spent all those years waiting at home for you?'

'I've always been faithful. I assumed she had.'

'Even Mason knew about it.'

'How?'

'He kept his eyes open, I suppose. Maybe he wasn't as naïve as you. He was attempting to blackmail Fiona.'

'She never said anything.'

'What did you expect her to say? I'm sorry, but I've been screwing Geoff Pearson, and now Gordon Mason is trying to blackmail me into having sex with him.'

'Did she?'

'She said she did not.'

'Did she murder Gordon Mason?'

'According to the police, it seems unlikely. Whoever put the daggers into Mason would have had to have been on the stage. She could have been an accomplice.'

'With Pearson?'

'Len, how the hell do I know? I'm your brother, not your keeper. Do you think Fiona would be capable?'

'To protect her perfect life? She'd be capable of anything.'

'Even the murder of Gordon Mason, of Geoff Pearson?'

'Yes.'

'Whatever you do, don't tell the police of your suspicions. They've got enough to convict her.'

'For what? Pearson fell to his death.'

'A long way. He may not have died; she may not have known the wall was there.'

'It's not murder then?'

'The police will make sure the case is tight. If they can tie her in with Mason's death, then it will not look good for her.'

'I need to see her,' Len Dowling said.

'Are you capable of murder, Len?'

'Why me? I'm the wronged party here. I'm the one with the cheating wife.'

'If you had known, what would you have done?'

'I would have forgiven her.'

'Why?'

'Because I love her.'

'After what she's done?'

'I can forgive, I can't replace.'

'Len, you're a weak excuse for a man.'

'What would you have done?'

'I'd have beaten the living daylights out of her, and made sure that Pearson never walked again.'

'And Gordon Mason?'

'That bastard. He would have had an accident.'

'Maybe you killed him.'

'Why? He had nothing on me, only you. And besides, I want my money from your business within forty-eight hours.'

'Will you defend Fiona?'

'I'll do that once you've paid me the money.'

'I need longer.'

'Forty-eight hours.'

'You're a bastard, Chris.'

'I know it, and I'm proud of it. Just because I have a snivelling weasel of a brother doesn't mean I have to be like him.'

Chapter 19

Tremayne came into the office later in the morning. Clare could see that he was not well. 'What is it, guv?'

'I had trouble sleeping, nothing more.'

The man did look tired, not surprising given the long night that they had just endured. She said no more on the subject.

'Pearson's family?' Tremayne asked.

'His father will conduct a formal identification today.'

'Fiona Dowling?'

'Cheryl Pearson is with her.'

'Is that wise?'

'I've ensured a constable is present.'

'Fair enough. And the husband?'

'He's not been here yet.'

'Was Pearson one of the murderers?'

'It seems possible, although Mason's blackmailing of Fiona Dowling was none of his concern. He was a young man with a married woman. Nobody is going to criticise him; his friends will probably buy him a drink. If Mason knew, it was not a motive.'

'Fiona couldn't have killed the man, but someone could on her behalf.'

'There'd still need to be two.'

'We've always assumed that.'

'Could it be only one?'

'Not in the assassination scene.'

'It's bizarre,' Clare said.

'But why the stage? And then why does Fiona Dowling confront Pearson when we're not far away?'

'Pearson's death could still have been an unfortunate accident. Fiona's angry, the man has turned her over for a young and innocent girl. She's feeling her age, realising that her life is not as perfect as she likes to portray. She stalks Pearson, hoping to confront him with his girlfriend, to intimidate him and to scare her off, to convince Pearson that she needs him and that she can care for him.'

'That wasn't the story we got from Fiona Dowling,' Tremayne said.

'No woman wants to admit that she's getting old, that she can't turn a man's head.'

'And that would be important to her?'

'Critical, I'd say. It would be a motive for a confrontation, for violence if she lashed out. I don't believe that she intended to kill him. She had no issue with hitting him or the girlfriend, but it wasn't murder. The charge won't stick.'

'Are you saying that we should release her?'

'What can you charge her with, assault occasioning actual bodily harm?'

'Not really. If she had hit Pearson or the girlfriend out of anger or jealousy, it's not a custodial sentence. She'd be bound over by a magistrate to keep her distance, maintain the peace, probably some community service and anger management.'

***

Fiona Dowling and Cheryl Pearson sat across from each other in a small room. A policewoman stood to one side at a discreet distance. It was not the first time in a police station for Cheryl, as she'd spent the occasional night in the cells for committing an affray, the result of too much alcohol. For Fiona, it was a new experience. The two women held hands across the table.

'You should have told me that Gordon knew,' Cheryl said.

'You knew about Geoff and me?' Fiona said. She was still wearing the same clothes from the night before.

'I saw you with him.'

'Where?'

'In your house. Both of you were on the floor.'

'And you didn't tell me?'

'What was there to tell? You're my oldest friend. I wasn't passing judgement, and I wasn't about to tell anyone.'

158

'Gary?'

'He knows, but he'll never tell anyone.'

'And Geoff?'

'He saw me when you two were on the floor. Believe me, you weren't focussing by then.'

'You must think me an awful tart,' Fiona Dowling said.

'We've both been tarts in our day. I've worked it out of my system, you haven't.'

'I didn't mean to kill Geoff. I was angry, hurt.'

'How did Gordon find out?'

'I've no idea. Geoff wouldn't have told anyone.'

'I couldn't get him to talk about it afterwards,' Cheryl said.

'You tried?'

'We used to tease him. Sorry, it was at your expense, but he never said anything, and he wouldn't have told Gordon.'

'Then who else would have known?'

'Did Len ever suspect?'

'Never. It's not been good between us for some years, but Len is not the jealous type. He wouldn't have known about Geoff.'

'Were there others?'

'Geoff was the only one. It's not always been easy. Len is not the great lover.'

'I remember that.'

'You've slept with him?'

'You know I did. The week before you latched on to him.'

'We were terrible,' Fiona said. The first smile since Old Sarum crept across her face.

'It was fun, though,' Cheryl said. The women squeezed each other's hands. The policewoman looked, said nothing.

'I miss it sometimes.'

'You've chosen your life, I've chosen mine. I may have a unambitious man, a lousy job, and a disgusting place to live, but I'm happier than you.'

'If I get out of here, I'll follow your example,' Fiona said.

'Don't make promises you won't keep. If you walk away from here, you'll either stay in Salisbury or you won't, you'll stay with Len, or you won't, but in a couple of years, you'll have your social set and your perfect life. For me, I'll marry Gary and keep him happy. He can stay just the way he is.'

'You're a true friend,' Fiona said.

'Not good enough to introduce to your social set.'

'None of them will be down here to visit me. I'll be a parasite once the news of Geoff's death becomes public knowledge.'

'What are you going to do about Len?'

'I'll fix it up with him somehow. He's the one constant, even if he can be a pain sometimes.'

'And lousy in bed,' Cheryl added. 'You can always take another lover.'

'Not again. I've learnt my lesson there.'

The two women parted. Len, Fiona's husband, was outside and wanting to talk to his wife.

Cheryl left the room, smiled at Len as she walked past him. He glanced over at her and gave a weak smile, the only recognition he was capable of. Cheryl knew of two certainties: Fiona, her friend, would survive regardless, and that she'd find another man if it were necessary.

***

Jimmy Francombe had skipped school, and Trevor Winston had left his salon for his assistant to run. Gary Barker was not present, as he already knew the news. Phillip Dennison was due shortly. Peter Freestone, a busy man that day, had put his work to one side. The situation was grim.

The men sat in Freestone's office. It was still early, and the news had not permeated through the city. 'Geoff Pearson died last night,' Freestone said.

'What!' Jimmy Francombe said.

'After you left, his body was found near the old cathedral. If you know it, there's some of the original building and a drop to one side.'

'I know it,' Dennison said, as he came in the door.

160

'So do I,' Francombe said.

'Not me, but carry on,' Winston said. 'What were you saying about Geoff?'

'Geoff Pearson fell over the drop and was killed.'

'Are you certain?' Dennison asked.

'I was there. I saw his body. Fiona Dowling has been arrested.'

'On what charge?'

'Murder.'

'But why?'

'She's admitted to an altercation with him.'

'Why would Fiona fight with Geoff? I always thought they were friendly,' Winston said. 'She used to come into my salon. She only had good words to say about him, about all of us.'

'The police will probably want to interview us again.'

'Why?'

'We were there at their re-enactment and went home,' Dennison said.

'There's still the matter of Gordon Mason.'

'Did Geoff kill him? Is that the reason Fiona argued with him?' Winston asked.

'Are you kidding?' Francombe said. 'She hated Mason, more than any of us.'

'Hate. That's a strong word.'

'Dislike, not hate.'

'Did you hate Mason?' Freestone asked.

'Okay,' Francombe admitted, 'I hated the man with his snide remarks.'

'Enough to kill him?' Dennison asked.

'Why me? He fancied your wife. I saw you and Mason outside. I saw you hit him.'

'Is that correct?' Winston asked.

'He made an inappropriate comment about Samantha,' Dennison said.

'He made inappropriate comments about everyone, especially me,' Winston said.

'I may have hit him, but I didn't kill him.'

'How do we know?' Freestone asked.

'You've not answered why Fiona was arguing with Geoff,' Dennison said.

'They were involved.'

'An affair?' Winston said.

'Good old Geoff,' Francombe said.

'He may have been good old Geoff to you, but the man's dead as a result,' Freestone said. 'Did anyone else know about this?'

'She always had eyes for him, but Len was always there. I assumed that was all it was,' Winston said.

'Apparently not. I don't know the full story, only snippets from what I gleaned up at Old Sarum. No doubt the police will know a lot more.'

'If Geoff was one of the murderers, that still means that one of us is guilty,' Winston said. 'Who is it? And why are we meeting here? One of you could take out a knife now and stab us.'

'Get real, Trevor,' Dennison said. 'I don't know how it was done, but it wasn't any of us.'

'Can you be sure?' Freestone said.

'I am.'

'Why?'

'None of you have the nerve.'

'Gary Barker and Bill Ford are not here.'

'Maybe Gary, maybe Bill.'

'I don't believe it,' Freestone said.

'I'm leaving, important issues to deal with,' Dennison said.

'Was Geoff messing around with your wife as well?' Winston asked.

Dennison, a man angered by his financial losses and by his wife's behaviour, lunged forward at the hairdresser, striking him across the face.

'Back off, Dennison. Trevor's winding you up. You know he's a mincing little queer,' Freestone said.

'I'll not have anyone making comments about my wife,' Dennison said.

'If you don't want comments, then don't let her parade herself in public half-undressed. She's got a reputation as it is,' Winston said, cowering in a corner of the room.

'I've heard the rumours,' Jimmy Francombe said.

'You little bastard. I'll get you for that,' Dennison said, freeing himself from Freestone's grip. He grabbed the young man and smashed his head against the wall. He then stormed out of the room.

Winston moved over to Francombe, took a handkerchief out of his pocket and attempted to wipe away the blood. 'You'll need some stitches there.'

'That man could kill,' Freestone said. 'We need to tell the police.'

'You can deal with it,' Winston said. 'I'm taking Jimmy to the doctor's.'

***

Len Dowling sat across from his wife in the small room at the police station. Fiona Dowling avoided his gaze, her head held low. 'It was an accident,' she said.

'You were screwing him,' Len Dowling said.

'I made a mistake.'

'You've made me look a fool. How am I going to continue in this city?'

'Is that all you're concerned about, your precious reputation? What about the fact that I was having an affair? Doesn't that upset you?'

Both of them were on their feet. 'I'm sorry, you'll both have to sit down or I'll terminate this meeting,' the policewoman said.

'It won't happen again,' Fiona said, resuming her seat. Her husband sat down at the same time.

'I knew that you fancied him,' Len said.

'Why didn't you say something?'

'Such as?'

'That you loved me and that you didn't want me making a fool of myself.'

'Why? It's you who wears the trousers in our house.'

'That's a terrible comment. I've always supported you, driven you on to better things.'

'And screwed around in the meantime, while pretending to your friends. You're no better than Cheryl. Just a pair of tarts.'

'She has been here. She came as a friend, wanting to help. She didn't come here as judge and jury, ready to condemn without a trial.'

'What trial? Chris was here when you told the police about getting together with Pearson, your little trysts in our house, the back of the Range Rover.'

'I've never told them that. How do you know the details?'

'I'm not a total fool,' Len Dowling admitted.

'You knew all along? What kind of man are you? What kind of husband? You could have stopped it, given Geoff a good thumping, but what did you do? Nothing, that's what.'

'At least you left me alone.'

'To do what? Sell more houses? Screw the women in the office?'

'Would you have cared?'

'Of course I would have cared. I want a man, not an excuse. I want a man to love me, to protect me, to care for me.'

'Don't give me that crap, Fiona. You're in here feeling sorry for yourself, looking at spending a few years in jail for murdering your lover.'

'He wasn't my lover. He'd ended the relationship.'

'You couldn't keep him satisfied. That's why he had the young woman with him. He needed someone younger, firmer, not sagging around the edges. Admit it, Fiona, you're past it.'

'You bastard.' The two of them were on their feet. Fiona slapped her husband across the face; Len Dowling punched his wife. The policewoman pressed a bell; two police officers came in and separated the warring couple. The policewoman took hold of Fiona Dowling and escorted her back to her cell, arranging for a doctor to visit and check her condition after the punch. Len Dowling was led out to another room to cool down.

Chapter 20

Cheryl, oblivious to the events at Bemerton Road Police Station, headed out to the garden centre to see Gary. She realised that it was against her better judgement and she should have phoned, although when Gary was working he always left his phone in his other clothes, having changed into more suitable gardening wear.

'You shouldn't be here,' Gary said. 'If they see you…'

'They can go to hell for once. I've met Fiona.'

'How is she?'

'As you'd expect. I've also spoken to Sergeant Yarwood.'

'Is there any reason that you're telling me this now?'

'Gordon Mason knew about Fiona and Geoff. He was attempting to blackmail her.'

'Money?'

'No. He wanted to sleep with her.'

'Did he?'

'Fiona said no. I believe her.'

'How did Mason find out?'

'I never told him, and I trust you, Gary.'

'Then he either saw them together, or Geoff told him.'

'Unless someone else knew.'

'This is all too complicated for me,' Gary said. 'Just give me my plants and the soil, and I don't want any more.'

'That's why I love you,' Cheryl said. 'Fiona can have her action man; I'll take you.'

'I can be all action.'

'In that bedsit, I know you can.'

Gary looked up, could see his father coming over. 'You'd better make yourself scarce.'

'Not today, I'm not. I've had to see my oldest friend arrested, a friend of ours killed. Your parents can go to hell.'

'You're not welcome here. This is private property,' Gary's father said. Cheryl could see that he was puffing, even after walking the short distance from the office to where she stood with Gary.

'The sign out the front says open 9 a.m. to 5 p.m. I'm here as a member of the general public.'

'Not to us, you're not. You're just a shameless hussy aiming to take our Gary from us.'

'From what I can see, it'll be your maker taking you first.'

Gary Barker stood to one side, observing the spectacle. He'd taken enough abuse from them over the years. It was good to see them getting some back.

'How dare you mock the Lord.'

'I could tell you more about your religion than you'll ever know. You're a hypocritical bastard, you and that fool Mason.'

'Gordon Mason was a God-fearing man.'

'He was a misogynist bigot. I assume you know what a misogynist is?'

'Don't get smart with me. Get off my property.'

'It'll be Gary's soon.'

'You can't wait, can you, to get your hands on his money?'

'I can get my hands on him anytime. His money's not important, although we'll gladly accept it.'

'Over my dead body, it'll be.'

'Not long to go then,' Cheryl said.

'You'd better go, Cheryl,' Gary said.

'I'm off. See you later, lover.'

The two lovers shared a passionate kiss and embrace in front of the father. The man seethed. For once, Gary was not concerned.

***

Phillip Dennison arrived home to find his wife sitting quietly in one corner of the sitting room; she was reading a book. 'You're not going out?' he said.

'Looking like this?'

'No one will notice.'

'A black eye and a cut lip, they will.'

Dennison was in a good mood. He had checked his latest trades on the drive back from Freestone's office to the house: his luck had changed and he had recouped his losses. Also, his wife had received what was long overdue: a good beating.

It had been the same with his previous women. At first, they were grateful they had been lifted from the mediocrity of an office or a shop, the mediocrity of men with no money, the mediocrity of suburbia. With them, as with Samantha, their gratitude had lasted for a few months, a few years, and then came the demand for a better life, the ability to forget where they had come from, and then they were off and spending, not willing to give him the time he required.

With Samantha, he felt an affinity, a desire to keep her, but they had come at a cost. He had had to threaten her with a letter from Chris Dowling, a couple of smacks across the face, and the separation from her beloved Aston Martin. He hoped it was sufficient.

'We're going out tonight,' he said.

'What for?' the woman replied, without much enthusiasm.

'To celebrate. Our troubles are over.'

'What do you mean?'

'It doesn't matter. I want you to stay, that's all.'

'I'll try to be more careful in future,' Samantha said.

Phillip Dennison knew she would not, but it did not matter. A solution had been found, not of his own doing. From now on, he'd keep a watch on his wife. If she stepped out of line, then he knew the answer. If she considered being unfaithful in future, then he would know how to stop it. He thanked Fiona Dowling for inadvertently providing the solution.

***

Peter Freestone visited Bill Ford at his place of work. The man, as usual, was busy. 'You didn't meet with us,' Freestone said.

'Geoff Pearson's dead,' Ford said.

'Len Dowling must have known about him and Fiona.'

'Did you?'

'I've known Fiona a long time. The woman has needs. Len's a braggart, not much substance,' Ford said.

'You know Fiona better than I do.'

'I do. And Cheryl.'

'Did Geoff Pearson kill Mason?'

'For what reason? Geoff may have been playing with fire, but I don't see him killing the man.'

'Mason may have known about him and Fiona.'

'He may have, but Geoff was a young guy making out with an older woman. It's not something for him to worry about. Fiona would have been more concerned to keep the relationship secret, but as I said, I've known her a long time. She's smart, weighs up the pros and cons.'

'The police said that Pearson's death may have been an accident,' Freestone said.

'She'd be capable of anything to protect her life. Back when she was younger, she enticed Cheryl into our bed.'

'Why are you telling me this?'

'I know you'll keep it confidential. What Fiona wants, she gets.'

'You think she'll get off a murder charge?'

'We've walked around the old cathedral in the past, you and I. Maybe she pushed him, a gentle shove, slap around the face, or maybe she pushed him hard.'

'We'll never know, nor will the police.'

'She couldn't have killed Gordon Mason.'

'I agree with you on that. If there were two men on that stage, then two had a reason. I wouldn't discount Fiona having some involvement, even if it was in the background.'

'Len?'

'It's possible.'

'Jimmy Francombe, Gary Barker, Trevor Winston?'

'Even us two,' Bill Ford said.

'It's not one of us,' Freestone said.

'Why?'

'I've no reason to kill him.'

'Would you know if you had stabbed him with a real dagger?'

'I'm certain I would have. And besides, he was still alive when he staggered over to me.'

'I know that, so do the police.'

'But he spoke?'

'Did he? You could have uttered the line. Would anyone have known?'

'Bill, you've spent too long in here with these bodies. That's just fanciful nonsense. I had no reason to kill him, and I was not after Fiona or Dennison's wife. I've been happily married for too long.'

'So you keep telling us. Are you trying to convince yourself, or did you fancy Fiona? She's a good-looking woman, and Dennison's wife is a knockout. I fancied her, I know that.'

'I thought you were a one-woman man?'

'I was,' Ford said, 'but the nights get lonely sometimes.'

'Get out of this place,' Freestone said. 'It's making you crazy.'

'Maybe it is, but I have my suspicions.'

'What are they?'

'I'll keep them to myself for now.'

***

Fiona Dowling, finally released on her own surety, retreated to her house. Tremayne still had his suspicions that she had known what she was doing, and there had been some moonlight that night.

Superintendent Moulton was suitably displeased at what had happened, as one murderer had been better than none. It was clear that Pearson's death, unfortunate as it was, was not related to the primary death of Gordon Mason. Pearson, whereas he may have been involved in the murder of Gordon Mason, had not died as a result of that, although knowledge of his affair may well have been the catalyst for Mason's death.

170

Clare was willing to give Fiona Dowling the benefit of the doubt, as in her teens she had experienced the anguish of being discarded by a young man at her school. She had not contemplated either hitting him or pushing him to his death, but she remembered the hurt she had felt. Fiona Dowling was married, supposedly happily, but then, Clare wondered, what was happiness: an illusion or was it tangible? She had felt happiness with Harry, but would it have been eternal, or was that just a fleeting fancy?

She realised that she had been in mourning for long enough. It was time to embrace the world again; hopefully to find love.

Fiona Dowling, keeping a low profile after her release, was quiet for a few days. The local newspaper had recorded Pearson's death as an accident, and it was likely that the coroner would as well, the altercation mentioned but not deemed relevant. There'd be an inquest, but it would not last long. Jim Hughes, in his role as the crime scene examiner, would be required to give evidence. His report had shown that there was clear evidence of two people standing on the lip of the drop and that the shoe prints indicated that one was facing towards the other in a stance that was suspicious. Apart from that, there was no proof. The woman, her shoe prints checked and found to match those at the scene, would be required to give evidence. Clare wondered how she'd be able to square that with her friends, although she assumed she would.

After an absence of a few days, Len Dowling was back in his office, his agency signs visible around the city. Clare had received a price for the cottage she had been leasing in Stratford sub Castle. The purchase would not need Dowling, and she was anxious to keep his grubby hands away from the deal.

The Deer's Head, Harry's pub, reopened with the appropriate fanfare. Neither Tremayne nor Clare attended the ceremony, although Clare realised that she could drive past the place without feeling the tears welling up in her eyes.

Eventually, Fiona Dowling reappeared in the city. Clare first saw her in Guildhall Square parking her car, and then she was at Winston's getting her hair done. From what Clare could see, the woman was without shame. The dramatic society knew about her affair, as did her husband, and no doubt there were others.

Clare decided a visit to the woman's house was in order. 'I've just a few questions,' she said, after being invited in.

'I've moved on from Old Sarum.'

'You've admitted to an altercation.'

'Yes.'

'How have you explained that to your friends?'

'They understand.'

'Understand what? That you had an argument with your ex-lover?'

'It gives me a sense of mystique.'

'If they accept that, then they're not worth your time.'

'You'll not understand. I need them, even if they are vacuous and empty-headed.'

'And loaded with money.'

'As you say, loaded with money. Cheryl may be willing to live like a pauper, I'm not.'

'Your husband's business?'

'It's doing well.'

'And your husband?'

'He understands.'

'Is he willing to accept that you were having sexual relations with another man?'

'He was angry, but I've fixed it with him.'

'How?'

'I've promised to devote myself to him.'

'Will you?'

'He's a weak man. He needs a strong woman. Whatever I say, he will agree.'

'Even if it's not true.'

'Even then.'

'Did Geoff Pearson kill Gordon Mason to protect you?'

'I didn't need his help.'

'Did he know that Mason was trying to blackmail you?'

172

'I never told him. I don't need a man to do my dirty work. If Mason had persisted, I would have dealt with him.'

'Murder?'

'Not murder. The man may have convinced other people that he was honest, but I knew him for the charlatan that he was.'

'Will it implicate your husband? Is it to do with the land deal?'

'It cannot be proved.'

'We've found no evidence.'

'You won't. And besides, I've no intention of telling you any more.'

'Why did you tell me?'

'I don't know. Maybe I'm upset by recent events. Maybe I needed to clear my conscience.'

'Or maybe you want to pre-empt my questioning, knowing full well that you knew about the drop over the side of the old cathedral at Old Sarum, that you wanted Geoff Pearson dead for the hurt he had caused you. Is this talk of Mason's blackmail just a red herring, aiming to divert the blame from you? To make you look like the victim instead of the villain? Mrs Dowling, I put it to you, that you murdered Geoff Pearson for no other reason than anger at the man who had spurned you.'

'That's a scurrilous lie. I invite you into my house, show you cordiality, and then you accuse me of murder.'

'Why not? You're a devious woman. You could have been the instigator of Mason's death, if not the person holding the dagger.'

'Leave, leave this house immediately. I will need to talk to my solicitor about this. I'm a private citizen being subjected to police brutality.'

'Mrs Dowling, this is not police brutality. And if you feel the need to take action, and we subsequently find you guilty of the murder of Geoff Pearson, and an accomplice in the murder of Gordon Mason, it will reflect badly on you.'

'It wasn't me.'

'What do you mean?'

'I didn't kill Gordon Mason. I wasn't involved.'

173

'Then who was?'
'I don't know.'

Chapter 21

Clare found Tremayne sitting at his desk on her return to the station. The man for once was quiet. 'What is it, guv?'

'This weekend. I'm meeting up with my ex-wife.'

'What's the problem?'

'I've been on my own for a long time. I'm used to doing as I please.'

'Too long being selfish. If you're both free, both lonely, then there's no harm done?'

'I'm not lonely.'

'Of course you are. What have you got in your life? A television, a pint of beer, a few old horses that can barely run, and me.'

'You?'

'This department then. You're getting on. It'll be good to have company.'

'For when I become old and senile, is that how you see it, Yarwood? You and Moulton, both of you see me as past it.'

'A little bit of fire there, guv.'

'Are you winding me up?'

'You know I am. Anyway, we need to talk.'

'About what?'

'Fiona Dowling, the death of two members of the Salisbury Amateur Dramatic Society.'

'What about Fiona Dowling?'

'I've been to see her.'

'What does she have to say for herself.'

'She's a tough woman. If she had been on that stage, she could have killed him.'

'But she wasn't.'

Tremayne raised himself from his seat. Clare's comments had struck home. He was the person who created the action, not her. 'What's first, Yarwood?'

'Len Dowling. We need to understand the man. His wife has spent time in custody, has been accused of murder, and he must know that she had been sleeping with Pearson.'

'He'd be an odd individual if he accepted his wife sleeping around. Where is he?'

'We'll find him back at work.'

The two police officers left the police station, Tremayne driving for once.

They found the estate agent in his office. 'Mr Dowling, a few questions,' Tremayne said.

'Don't you ever give up? I've got a busy schedule,' Dowling said.

'So do we. We need to talk to you about your wife.'

'She's at home. You can talk to her there.'

'It's your views that are important.'

'Okay, twenty minutes.'

The three retreated to an office at the rear of the agency. Out front, three agents were on the phone or talking to anyone who walked through the door.

'Mr Dowling, your wife was arrested on suspicion of murder.'

'Yes, I know this.'

'Do you know why she was suspected?'

'If you want me to say that she was involved with Pearson, then I will.'

'Was she?'

'I know about it.'

'How do you feel that your wife is unfaithful?'

'What do you want me to say?'

'It's not what we want you to say. We want to know your reaction.'

'Angry, bloody angry. Does that satisfy you?'

'You're not very convincing,' Clare said. 'Did you know or did you suspect?'

'I know Fiona. I've always been hopeful that she'd stay faithful, but I've never been certain.'

'When it was confirmed, it did not come as a big shock.'

'It was a shock, but I was not surprised, or not much. No man wants to know that his wife is cheating, it's a blow to the ego, but I will tell you one thing, I will not give up on my wife.'

'Why?'

'Because I love her. We built this business up together, and she was here in the early days working horrendous hours. Our history runs deep, and if the cost is the occasional infatuation, then I must accept.'

'That's a magnanimous attitude,' Clare said.

'It's not magnanimous. It's the reality.'

'Were you aware that Gordon Mason was attempting to blackmail your wife?'

'No.'

'What would you have done if you had known?'

'Are you asking if I would have killed him?'

'Would you?'

'I would have threatened the man. I'd have asked my brother to pressure him.'

'And what does your brother think of your forgiving your wife?'

'I've not forgiven her; I've been forced to accept it.'

'Your brother?'

'He thinks I'm a fool and that I should get a backbone.'

'Do you agree with him?'

'He's right, no doubt, but I'm not going to give up on Fiona.'

'If you had known that Gordon Mason was pressuring your wife, that would be a motive for murder.'

'I didn't know, and I didn't kill Mason.'

Tremayne and Clare left the office, walking past Harry's old pub. They could see the patrons inside, a new publican behind the bar. Neither made a comment.

'Why would the woman continue to go to the rehearsals, take part in the play, if one of the men was blackmailing her? It makes no sense,' Tremayne said.

'You'd think she would have kept away,' Clare said.

'And even then, she was maintaining cordial relations with him.'

'Do you think she had given in to his demands?'

'With Fiona Dowling, who knows?'

***

Tremayne and Yarwood continued working the case, re-interviewing the main suspects, checking out Old Sarum, looking for an angle. Clare had to admit that the reduced pace in the department did not suit her. For a few weeks, she had been busy, close to exhaustion, which was how she had managed to handle the return to Salisbury, but now she had time to remember. Even driving down Minster Street and passing Harry's pub had proved to be painful. She wanted to visit his grave, but not yet.

Tremayne had met up with Jean, his former wife, and they had spent the weekend at a hotel not far from Salisbury. They had discussed getting together on a more regular basis, even a holiday overseas, anathema to Tremayne, but he had agreed. It would have to wait, though, until they had dealt with the murder of Gordon Mason.

Fiona Dowling almost revelled in her notoriety, of how she had risen from a foolish and then promiscuous schoolgirl to being the wife of Salisbury's leading estate agent. She had even agreed to make a speech on the subject at the next meeting of her group.

Len Dowling continued to sell residential property, even calling up Tremayne one Saturday morning with a firm buyer, and could he show them around his house. Tremayne made short work of his request, vowed to check out the man more intensely for his nerve in disturbing him after a few too many drinks the previous night.

Clare had managed to secure the finance for the cottage that she was leasing and the purchase was going through, no thanks to Dowling who had tried to scupper the deal by telling the vendor that he had a better offer. As it turned out the vendor had been a friend of Mavis Godwin, and she remembered Clare fondly. There was no way that she was going to let a slug of a man take the house from the police sergeant, the vendor's words not Clare's, although she had to agree with the woman.

Samantha Dennison had been seen around the town, back to driving the Aston Martin. Clare had seen her on a couple of occasions, had a coffee with her once. The woman was calmer than before, not as extravagant, judging by the reduced number of shopping bags.

Although a sense of normality reigned amongst those who had been up at Old Sarum that night, Tremayne was still biting at the bit. The man wasn't calm, far from it, and he was subject to the occasional bout of frustration, sometimes losing his cool with Clare.

Geoff Pearson had been laid to rest, the entire dramatic society present, apart from the Dowlings, and a verdict of death by misadventure recorded. Tremayne didn't hold with it, convinced that there was malice on Fiona Dowling's part, but he couldn't prove it.

Superintendent Moulton, continued with his attempts to retire Tremayne. The last time that it had been mentioned, Tremayne had told him what to do with it. The end result – an internal hearing as to why a detective inspector had instructed his superior what to do with his badgering. The Police Federation would deal with it on his behalf, although he knew he'd receive a warning. Tremayne knew his time was coming to an end, but not before he wrapped up the murder of Gordon Mason. For several days, he had mulled over what to do. He still had suspicions about Fiona Dowling and her husband, supposedly reconciled and openly affectionate. Gary Barker and Cheryl Milledge seemed to be innocent bystanders, and Bill Ford was a grave man, although Tremayne did not believe that his sedentary lifestyle and his bland countenance were all there was to the funeral director. He had admitted to being a passionate man in his youth, the threesome with Fiona and Cheryl testament to that fact, but now the man seemed to have little interest in life, other than spending time with the dead of the city and taking off to London every week or two.

Both Trevor Winston, a man who minced in his salon but not outside, and Jimmy Francombe, an enthusiastic thespian who had been drunk more than a few times around the city and suspended once from his school, seemed harmless to Tremayne.

Freestone seemed a more straightforward man to read, more Tremayne's age group, and the men shared similar tastes, similar vices. Freestone was not into horses, but he enjoyed a good smoke and a few too many beers on occasion.

***

Time had moved on, too slowly for Tremayne. The man liked being busy, Clare could see that, and for weeks there had been no progress. Sure, the paperwork was up to date, but with no clear direction on how to move the investigation forward. Even interviewing those who had been present that night in Old Sarum had run its course. There still remained the fact that seven men alive and one dead included two murderers, but a tie-in between any two of them was tenuous. Apart from a possible rezoning that was not above board, none of the other conspirators was visibly linked.

Bill Ford and Peter Freestone were friendly, but Freestone only had one stab at the man, whereas Ford would have had plenty. Even that, Tremayne felt, was not sufficient grounds to murder Mason, and besides, Ford was a funeral director, he was financially sound, and was only interested in maintaining the family business.

And why, Tremayne wondered, did anyone want to risk being caught, spending time in prison? And again, why on a stage? It seemed ghoulish to him, as if the persons responsible not only wanted the man dead, they also wanted the notoriety of the unsolved murder, being the unknown assailant. It seemed strange to Tremayne, but then he had dealt with worshippers of ancient gods and human sacrifices in his time, and nothing would surprise him now.

The death of Bill Ford did, though. It was four in the afternoon when the call came through. Clare was in the office. 'Yarwood, get your coat,' Tremayne said.

'What's happened?'

'Another murder.'

'Someone we know?'

'Bill Ford.'

Upon their arrival, they found a distraught man standing outside in the reception area of the funeral home. 'I found him,' he said.

Clare assumed he was there for a loved one. He would need to be interviewed later.

In the room at the back, the same place where they had spoken with Ford before, they found the man lying in a coffin, his arms folded across his front.

'Someone needs psychiatric help,' Tremayne said.

Clare could see what he meant. In the man's chest was a Roman dagger. 'It's more than blackmail,' she said.

'We've been looking for a motive, but it's been the wrong motive.'

Around them, the crime scene team were filing in. Outside, in the reception area and on the street, the uniforms were following procedure. Inside, Clare and Tremayne moved closer to the body. 'It's a crime scene,' Jim Hughes said. 'Where's your protective gear?'

'Sorry, we've just arrived, the same as you,' Tremayne said.

'I understand that, but from here on, it's my show. I'll let you know what I find.'

'It's clear what happened here.'

'There's no sign of a struggle, a dagger in the heart. It's murder,' Hughes said.

'We'd figured that out.'

Tremayne and Clare sat down next to the man in reception. 'I came to organise the burial of my wife,' he said.

Clare could see that the man was elderly, and grieving. 'I'm sorry for your loss. Can you tell us what happened here?'

'I came here to check with Mr Ford that all was in order. There wasn't anyone at the front, so I walked around to the back. I knew where my wife was as I had been here before. I found Mr Ford lying in one of the coffins. That's all I can tell you.'

Tremayne realised that the man had nothing to do with the crime. 'We'll need a written statement. Apart from that, you're free to leave.'

'What for? My wife is here. The burial is tomorrow.'

'It's a crime scene. I suggest you contact another funeral director, and I'll see if your wife's body can be released to you.'

'Thank you. Can I see my wife before I leave?'

'I'll get you a set of crime scene protective gear.'

***

With little more to be achieved, and pending Jim Hughes's report, Tremayne and Clare returned to the police station. Tremayne phoned Peter Freestone, made sure that he was available for further questioning.

'You place a lot of reliance on that man,' Clare said.

'Not totally, but the man is observant. Bill Ford has been killed for a reason. We assume it's related to what happened at Old Sarum.'

'It's a Roman dagger.'

'Precisely, which means there are more than the two with metal blades that we originally assumed.'

'It's three now. How many more are there?'

'It's impossible to say. We weren't able to trace where the blades came from, nor the extra daggers.'

Freestone arrived at Bemerton Road Police Station within the hour; the man was distraught. 'This means something else, doesn't it?' he said to Tremayne. They were sitting in Tremayne's office, Clare as well.

'We've assumed that the motive was tangible,' Tremayne said.

'What do you mean?'

'Gordon Mason was as a result of blackmail, or he knew something, threatened to talk. The latter of those two being the land deal.'

'The first?' Freestone asked.

'Fiona Dowling and her relationship with Geoff Pearson.'

'Why did Geoff Pearson die? Was it murder?'

'Fiona Dowling admitted to the altercation, although she didn't stay around at the site after Pearson's death, suspicious in itself but not conclusive.'

'Then why Bill Ford?' Freestone asked.

'Our investigations have shown nothing against the man. He led a solitary life, he'd admitted to knowing Fiona and Cheryl when they were younger. He's not been involved in any criminal or dubious activities to our knowledge, and if he had known about Fiona Dowling and Pearson, he did not seem to be a man who'd use it to his advantage.'

'So why is he murdered?'

'And why is he placed in a coffin, his arms folded?' Tremayne said.

'Someone with a sense of the macabre,' Clare said.

'Or someone who enjoys murder,' Tremayne said.

'Whoever it is, he could be after me,' Freestone said.

'Even us,' Clare said. 'This person is obviously unhinged, and he's probably one of those on the stage that night.'

'That only leaves Jimmy, Gary, Trevor, Phillip and me,' Freestone said.

'Who else would know where to buy the retractable daggers?' Clare asked.

'It was no secret. I sent out a monthly report on the finances of the dramatic society. The information is all there,' Freestone said.

'If we discount you for the moment,' Tremayne said.

'For the moment? Am I still a suspect?'

'I can't negate the possibility.'

'We've been through this before,' Freestone said.

Clare could see that the man was not comfortable in the police station. She left and went to get him a cup of tea in an attempt to calm his nerves.

'It could be me next,' Freestone said.

'As well as Yarwood and myself.'

'What causes people to commit such acts?'

'You'd need someone other than me to answer that, but now I'm willing to concede that Bill Ford's murder is as a result of a disturbed personality, not as a result of a tangible motive.'

'You mean that this person is avenging the death of Caesar?'

'Why not?'

'Then it could be any of us five,' Freestone said.

Clare returned and gave a cup of tea to Freestone, another to Tremayne. 'What's the plan, guv?' she asked.

'Interview the main suspects again.'

'And the two women?'

'Would they have had the strength to place Ford's body in the coffin?'

'Cheryl Milledge may have.'

Chapter 22

A few days after Bill Ford's death, the primary suspects met in Len Dowling's office. It was after seven in the evening when all those involved arrived. First at the office was Phillip Dennison, this time with Samantha. Soon after came Jimmy Francombe and Trevor Winston, and ten minutes later Peter Freestone, Gary Barker, and Cheryl Milledge. Fiona Dowling was already there with her husband.

'What is it, Freestone?' Len Dowling asked.

'I thought that was obvious.'

'One of us is a murderer, is that it?'

'Precisely. Bill Ford was an innocent bystander. The man wasn't having an affair with your wife or insulting Dennison's. On the contrary, the man always behaved impeccably.'

'How dare you disrespect my wife,' Dowling said.

Dennison could see the evening getting out of control. 'It doesn't help, trading insults,' he said.

'I'm not insulting anyone,' Freestone said. Everyone was sitting down, all a little nervous as to what was happening to the group that had once met out of love for acting, but was now meeting to discuss a murderer.

'It sounded that way to me,' Dowling said.

'Sit down, Len,' Fiona Dowling said. 'Let Peter talk.'

'Thank you, Fiona. As I was saying, there were a number of motives for Mason's murder. Maybe they weren't sufficient to justify the taking of a life, but they were there.'

'Get to the point,' Dowling said.

'The point is that one of us seems to enjoy murder. None of us is safe.'

'Did you see Ford's body?'

'No, but I've seen a photo. It was one of the daggers.'

'If someone killed Bill Ford, it must be because they had a reason,' Cheryl said.

'That's an assumption. What I am saying is that someone is killing us off. Even if Geoff Pearson was one of those on the stage with a lethal weapon, there is still the fact that someone else is still alive. There are nine people here. One of this nine murdered Bill Ford.'

'Are you suggesting that this person intends to kill us all?' Dennison asked.

'Why am I here?' Samantha Dennison asked.

'I'm sorry to say it, but your husband had a reason to dislike Gordon Mason, and you've become involved in our group by default. If your husband is not the murderer–'

'I'm not.' Dennison defended his position.

'–if your husband is not the murderer,' Freestone continued after the interruption, 'then it is still feasible that someone else killed him on your behalf, or maybe it was someone defending Fiona's honour.'

'I don't get what you're trying to say,' Dowling said. 'You insult my wife, accuse Dennison of murder. Is that all this is tonight, a chance to vent your spleen, to take control of us the way you did the dramatic society?'

'Len, listen to what I'm saying. There are nine here, and one of us is a murderer. That leaves eight people still alive. What if this person is determined to keep murdering? We are all potential victims.'

'It can't be Cheryl or me,' Fiona said.

'Why?'

'We weren't on the stage, we didn't plunge a dagger into him.'

'It doesn't need to be one of those on the stage, does it?' Samantha said. 'Any one of us could have killed Bill Ford.'

'At last the words of wisdom,' Freestone said. 'Samantha's right. We've always assumed that Bill Ford was innocent, in that he had no motive for Mason's death, but what if he did?'

'And someone else wanted to remove the only remaining link to him and the crime,' Gary Barker said.

'It's conjecture, but it's possible.'

'So who is it?' Jimmy Francombe asked.

'Let's analyse it.'

'That person could have a dagger with them now,' Winston said.

'He could,' Freestone replied.

'He?' Francombe said.

'Gordon Mason died at the hands of a man. Who killed Bill Ford is unclear. It could be a woman.'

'It's not me,' Fiona said.

'Nor me,' Cheryl added.

'Fiona and Cheryl, everyone in this room will declare their innocence,' Freestone said. 'The police cannot protect us, and they've no idea. It is up to us to protect ourselves.'

'What do you suggest?' Trevor Winston said.

'If everyone leaves Salisbury, then we're all safe.'

'I can't leave,' Dowling said.

'What do you suggest?' Winston said again.

'We could hold a murder mystery night.'

'When?'

'This week. We can meet at my house or Len and Fiona's.'

'We'll use my house,' Dennison said. 'Do we need a script?'

'We'll replay the events to date.'

'Are we involving the police?'

'I would suggest that DI Tremayne and Sergeant Yarwood are there.'

'Very well, this Friday at 8 p.m.'

***

Jim Hughes's report on Bill Ford's death had revealed little more of value. The man had died after being stabbed in the heart with a dagger. There was no sign of a struggle, and the one stab had resulted in a rapid blood loss.

'Whoever killed him cleaned up afterwards. The victim was a meticulous man, and he had sufficient cleaning materials,' Hughes said in Tremayne's office, a place that no longer held any fear for him since the CSE had gained the DI's hard-won respect.

'Male or female?'

'We're unable to tell you. Whoever it is, he's becoming smart.'

'He?'

'A figure of speech. It could be a female. Mind you, it would have been difficult for a woman to lift the victim into the coffin, but not impossible.'

'It's possible, though?'

'As I've said, I believe so. Who do you think is the murderer?'

'It's no clearer. Bill Ford was always seen as a neutral character: mild-mannered, polite, did not make scurrilous comments about the women, never attempted to force himself on them.'

'Not a bad word against him, is that it?' Hughes asked.

'That appears to be the consensus.'

'You believe the killer is deranged?'

'Or enjoying the notoriety.'

'There's no notoriety if you're not known.'

'Maybe they enjoy the fact that they committed the perfect crime.'

'In that they've stayed free.'

'That's it,' Tremayne said.

***

Tremayne always appreciated a working lunch at the Pheasant Inn in Salisbury. For once, Clare had accompanied him, even agreed to a glass of wine.

Peter Freestone was already there. He was a busy man, the same as the two police officers, and he needed to be back in his office within the hour.

'Do you have it?' Tremayne asked.

Freestone handed over the recording that he had taken at the meeting in his office with the remaining members of the dramatic society. 'Does that mean I'm no longer a suspect?' he asked.

188

'You're not high on my radar,' Tremayne replied as he drank his beer, almost downing the full pint in one gulp. 'I needed that,' he said.

Clare had no intention of drinking more than the one glass of wine, and she was drinking it slowly.

'It's all arranged. This Friday night, eight in the evening, Dennison's house.'

'They've agreed to my idea?' Tremayne said.

'Whoever this person is they certainly have some nerve,' Freestone said.

'He's enjoying it, or maybe it's a she.'

'And you've no idea?'

'Motives, but no proof.'

'Did Fiona kill Geoff Pearson?'

'Unless she admits her guilt, there's no way we can prove it. You've been up there at night.'

'I still think it was intentional to push him over,' Clare said.

'Death was never certain,' Freestone said as he ate his steak. Tremayne had ordered a steak, as well; Clare, a salad.

'Agreed. It depends on how hard she pushed him. Maybe she just wanted to hurt him, but she's out and about, somewhat of a heroine with her friends.'

'Not my kind of friends,' Clare said.

Tremayne ordered another pint, as did Freestone. Clare could see that the two men were firm friends, although one may have to arrest the other before the week was out. She continued to eat her salad, listening to the two men as they talked.

Clare had to acknowledge the similarities in the two men: both were in their fifties, both dressed in a similar manner, almost could have passed as brothers, although Freestone was at least six inches shorter than Tremayne.

'We'll run through the chain of events, the motives of each, the truth.'

'Geoff Pearson and Dowling's wife?'

'Everything. Even Cheryl Milledge and her past, Gary Barker and the garden centre.'

'What about Winston's homosexuality, Jimmy Francombe's drunkenness of late?'

'Everything, warts and all. It's a murder enquiry, and I intend to wrap it up. If there is to be anger and embarrassment, then so be it.'

'Dennison and Samantha, and what Mason called her?'

'Everything. It's going to be a wild night. We're not going to leave there without an arrest,' Tremayne said. He ordered another beer; he was in no hurry to leave.

***

Tremayne was confident that a confrontation with all the possible suspects was the only solution. The case had dragged on too long, and as far as he could see, if the people remained in their comfort zones, there'd be no resolution, and it was a resolution that he needed. And then there was his ex-wife, Jean; they regularly spoke, almost as if they were in their twenties and newly in love, although Tremayne knew it wasn't love. However, the idea of companionship appealed, even if only on an occasional basis.

Jean had booked a trip to southern Spain in three weeks' time. He had looked it up on the internet. It looked hot, too hot for him, but they served beer there, and he had agreed. He never let on that he was pleased to be going, not to his wife who knew it would be out of character to show too much emotion, and not to Yarwood who would have a smart comment.

Tremayne knew he could only go if the current case were concluded, and he hoped the event scheduled for that Friday evening would give him a result. Clare, pleased to be busy, occupied herself with the preparations, compiling a scenario of how the night should unfold. She had struggled to reconcile herself with being back in Salisbury, but was finding it easier to deal with Harry's death, even considering a date with another police officer. She would not see it as anything other than a night out, and she wasn't sure about it, but she wanted to stay in the city with its history and its quaintness.

Her parents, especially her mother, continued to ask her to return to their hotel and Norfolk, but she knew she would not. Besides, it was only two weeks before she moved into her cottage, and she needed some time off to check out the local shops for furnishings.

Samantha Dennison was also occupied preparing for the evening, treating it as a social event rather than a police investigation. Clare hoped she wasn't involved, as she had grown to like the woman, a person who had been blunt in her evaluation of what she was. Her openness was refreshing compared to Fiona Dowling, who had complained about the way Clare had confronted her in her house. Police intimidation, verging on brutality, was how it was described in the letter from her brother-in-law, the solicitor Chris Dowling.

Clare had to credit Superintendent Moulton in his support for her. He had worded a reply to Chris Dowling, and ultimately to his client, that Sergeant Yarwood was well within her rights to question a suspect, to apply pressure if required, and that it was murder, not a minor misdemeanour. No more was heard on the matter and the next time that Clare had run into Fiona Dowling in the city centre, not difficult in a small city, the woman had been polite and friendly.

Tremayne called Clare into his office. The investigative team consisted of just the two of them, as since the death of Vic Oldfield, their previous constable, there had been no replacement. Just the two of them, supported by a group of diligent professionals in the office, suited Tremayne and Clare, but they knew it would not be long before they'd be asked to take on additional investigative staff if there were any new murder cases.

'Yarwood, are we ready?'

'For the Friday night?' Clare said. She could see that Tremayne was champing at the bit to get on.

'What else?'

'We'll be ready. Are we taking uniforms?'

'We'll have a police car outside in the driveway.'

'What are our chances of an arrest?' Clare asked.

191

'There'll be an arrest.'

'It could be the Dennisons.'

'No one is safe from our questioning, not even them. The fact that it's their house is inconsequential.'

Chapter 23

Phillip Dennison's house, large and expensively decorated, was welcoming on the Friday night. Clare had arrived early, Tremayne was due within twenty minutes. On the dining room table, a buffet was laid out.

Clare had to admit that if the night were purely social, then it would have been enjoyable. She wasn't sure if the dramatic society members understood the seriousness of the situation, as if they thought that Tremayne often took part in murder mystery nights, where amateur detectives dress up in Sherlock Holmes' deerstalkers and period costumes, and act out the murder and then attempt to solve it.

It was strange, she thought, that all those invited were excited to come, but then, she realised, they were imbued with the love of acting, and the murderer was apparently the most accomplished in avoiding detection. And as for those genuinely innocent, they had nothing to fear, only the joy of being present at the event.

Even Clare had to admit to some excitement in that she would be required to play a part: the good police officer to Tremayne's bad. One would be raising the heat, the other would be soothing, consoling, and gently pressuring to let the person confess.

Peter Freestone was the first member of the dramatic society to arrive, closely followed by Gary Barker and Cheryl Milledge. The others came soon after.

The main room of the house was to be the setting. Everyone helped themselves to the buffet, and the alcohol. Clare noticed that Tremayne kept to a soft drink.

'Ladies and gentlemen, I would like to offer our appreciation to Phillip and Samantha for making us all very welcome, but let me remind you that this is a police investigation, not a social gathering, and not something that anyone here should regard as frivolous. Sitting here in this room are two murderers.'

'What do you reckon, DI Tremayne?' Phillip Dennison asked. He was sitting on a sofa, his wife at his side.

'We assumed initially that Gordon Mason was killed as a result of something he knew. In truth, we were looking for a motive.'

'And now?'

'There is an unknown factor. The possibility that the murderer or murderers kill for pleasure, or for the gratification that they are able to commit the perfect crime in front of an audience, surrounded by fellow actors.'

'A sick individual,' Len Dowling said. He was sitting on the other side of the room to Dennison. His wife sat nearby, holding his hand.

'If I look around this room,' Tremayne said, 'I see no one that fits the description of sick or psychotic, quite the contrary, but believe me, someone here is in need of medical treatment.'

'Then why would they be here tonight?' Fiona Dowling asked.

'The perfect crime requires it to remain hidden under the most intense scrutiny. The person responsible is laughing at us, sneeringly hiding behind a look of innocence,' Tremayne said.

'How will you find this person?' Samantha Dennison asked.

'I won't. It's your murder mystery night. You will identify the culprit. We will conduct this along the lines of a fictitious murder mystery, except this time there are real murders, those of Gordon Mason and Bill Ford.'

'What about Geoff Pearson?' Jimmy Francombe asked. Fiona Dowling said nothing, just stared at the young man. Her husband sat impassively.

'Tonight, all facts relating to our murder enquiry will be revealed. Geoff Pearson's death has been evaluated. The reason for his being pushed is known to most of you here, probably all, as you have no doubt discussed the matter.'

'I object to you accusing my wife,' Len Dowling said.

'Let it go,' Dowling's wife said. 'If they don't know, then I'll tell them. I was having an affair with Geoff. He had dumped me, I was angry. I confronted him at Old Sarum, pushed him, wanted to hit him, but he fell to his death. I panicked and left the area. I'm guilty of stupidity, not murder.'

'Thank you, Mrs Dowling,' Tremayne said. 'There are others with facts that they would prefer not be revealed, but tonight no one will be spared.

'Why do we have to endure this?' Phillip Dennison said.

'You know the answer to your question.'

'Do I?'

'I'll explain so we are all clear where this night is heading. Gordon Mason has been murdered, so has Bill Ford. Geoff Pearson has died. We have possible motives for Mason's death, none for Bill Ford. Our investigation of Ford indicates no negative marks against his character, no dislike of the man, no behaviour on his part that could be regarded as offensive. If that is the case, then Bill Ford was innocent of any crime other than that he was a member of the Salisbury Amateur Dramatic Society and that he was one of the conspirators who stabbed Caesar. If that is the motive, then you all know what will happen next.'

'He intends to kill the remaining conspirators,' Freestone said.

'Exactly. Which one of you sitting here tonight will be the next to be stabbed in the heart? Does anyone want to question what we are trying to achieve here?'

No one spoke. All looked ready for the murder mystery to begin.

Clare stood up. 'This is a summary of the mystery. A Shakespearean tragedy, *Julius Caesar*, was being acted out by an amateur dramatic society. The crucial scene acted in front of an audience was where Julius Caesar is stabbed to death by the conspirators, seven in total. A fictional slaying in that the knives were meant to be retractable and plastic bladed, only two weren't. Of the seven conspirators, and the thirty-four stabs at the body on that stage, five stabs entered his body from two modified daggers.

'Gordon Mason who played Julius Caesar died on that night. Since then two of his assassins have also died, Geoff Pearson and Bill Ford. That only leaves Trevor Winston, Gary Barker, Jimmy Francombe, and Len Dowling alive.'

'Are you suggesting that those five are possible victims?' Cheryl Milledge asked.

'Or potential murderers,' Tremayne said.

'This is ludicrous,' Winston said. 'Why would anyone want to kill me?'

'Why is it ludicrous?' Clare asked. 'You're homosexual by your own admission, you were one of the conspirators.'

'But I'm harmless.'

'So was Bill Ford, unless anyone can tell us to the contrary.'

No one said anything. Tremayne looked around the room; he could see no facial expressions of someone trying to hide something. Cheryl Milledge excused herself and went and got some more food, as well as two cans of beer, one for her, one for Gary Barker.

'We need to discuss the motives for Gordon Mason's murder,' Clare said.

'Do we need to reveal everyone's dirty laundry?' Fiona Dowling asked.

'Unfortunately we must, unless you want to go home tonight wondering if your husband is next, or whether he's a murderer.'

'That's slanderous,' Len Dowling said.

'Dowling, shut up,' Dennison said. 'Tremayne and Yarwood are attempting to save us. Your bellyaching, your promiscuous wife, your lousy reputation are of little consequence.'

Dowling was up on his feet, heading over towards Dennison, ready to land a punch. Gary Barker interceded and pushed him back in his seat.

'Sit down,' Fiona whispered to her husband. 'The police are baiting us all, seeing who will react.'

'I'll not have you insulted,' Dowling said.

'Very chivalrous, no doubt, but it's a bit late in the day to defend my honour.'

'I could hardly do it while you were screwing Pearson, could I?'

'You bastard.'

'If you two have finished talking,' Freestone said, 'I'd like to hear what Sergeant Yarwood has in store for us tonight.'

Clare continued. 'There are some possible motives for wanting Mason dead. I will detail them, hopeful that no one will react vocally or violently. This is no time for false modesty or downright denials. The police work on facts, and I will reveal what we know, what we've investigated, and possibly what we conjecture.

'We became aware of a possible fraudulent land deal which pointed to Peter Freestone, Len Dowling, and Gordon Mason working in collusion.'

Freestone rose from his chair to comment. Clare ignored him. 'We have found no proof that fraud was committed. We know that Mason had often insulted Trevor Winston, made reference to his homosexuality. Also, Mason insulted Samantha Dennison, called her a tart.'

'He called me a prostitute, selling myself to a rich man,' Samantha said.

'As I was saying, Mason called Samantha Dennison a prostitute. Phillip Dennison confronted the man and hit him. And finally, we also know that Mason was attempting to blackmail Fiona Dowling over her affair with Geoff Pearson.'

'My bastard husband knew all along. It would have saved me screwing the odious man.'

Tremayne stood up, the others in the room focussed their attention on the woman's remarkable admission. 'Are you saying that you had sexual intercourse with Gordon Mason?'

'It's a night of truths, isn't it? I don't want to be the next victim of whoever killed Mason, although I wish it had been me. Of course I screwed him. The man was going to tell Len. That wasn't such a big deal, but Mason could have spread the gossip around the city.'

'And now everyone here will tell,' Cheryl said.

'What does it matter? And besides, the reaction has been exactly the opposite of what I expected. DI Tremayne, or was it Sergeant Yarwood, said it correctly when they called my friends vacuous and empty-headed. To them, I'm the fallen woman redeemed, the woman who stands by her man, the woman who will not fail.'

'It's a good enough motive for murder,' Cheryl said. 'You would have had no issue with killing Gordon Mason, nor Bill Ford if he found out. Were you screwing him as well?'

'Cheryl, please. I'm frightened of whoever this killer is, the same as everyone else here.'

Cheryl said nothing, nor did anyone else. Tremayne studied Fiona Dowling. He knew that she could have killed Mason and Ford, could have killed Pearson too, but that would require a confession.

'We cannot rule out either Geoff Pearson's or Bill Ford's involvement in the death of Gordon Mason, nor can we prove that whoever killed Ford was also one of Mason's murderers, but the connection is indisputable.'

But why Bill Ford?' Winston asked. 'He was a decent man.'

'There's one more motive that we need to mention,' Clare said. 'It may not be known that Gary Barker is to inherit his parents' garden centre. It may be that most of you do not know that where he works is his family's business. The bad relationship between parents and son is exacerbated by his relationship with Cheryl. They see their son as incapable, and Cheryl as manipulative, only using Gary as a means to get their property.'

'Their view of me is worse than that. They hate me with a passion,' Gary Barker said. 'My father is in the hospital now; he's unlikely to last the night.'

'You should be there,' Samantha said.

'If he was a decent father, then maybe, but he's not. He's a vindictive, evil-minded hypocrite, the same as Mason. It was Mason they were using to prevent my inheriting.'

'Did he succeed?' Francombe asked.

'No. It'll be mine within the week, and then I'll move in with Cheryl.'

'What about your mother?' Clare asked.

'You've never met her. The doctor wants to put her in a nursing home. She needs constant supervision for dementia. There's a place ready for her. She'll barely notice the change in surroundings.'

'That's callous,' Samantha said.

'After the way they treated me, the way they treated Cheryl?'

'It's a motive for wanting Gordon Mason dead,' Tremayne said.

'It's an excellent motive, but I'd not have killed him on that stage. And why? He'd lost, my parents had lost. Why would I destroy all that I have out of anger and hatred? The man's dead and good riddance to him. Tonight, after we find the murderer, I'll shake his hand and thank him.'

Clare looked over at Tremayne, who cocked his head slightly upwards in acknowledgement of what they had both seen and heard: a man who could have killed both Mason and Ford.

***

Tremayne knew he had emotions running high, exactly where he wanted them. 'Mr Dowling, it is time to evaluate you.'

'Why me? Just because I've got a slut of a wife doesn't mean I killed Mason.'

'I know about you and the woman in the office, the extended meetings,' Fiona Dowling said.

'That's lies. You may screw around, I don't.'

'Not up to it, is that it? Not from what I know. If you weren't so busy with her, then maybe I wouldn't have needed to screw Pearson and whoever else.'

'Whoever else?'

Tremayne knew that this was precisely what he wanted, the heated passion, the anger, the contradictory statements, and now he had the Dowlings opening up. He could see the others watching and enjoying the spectacle, but their time was coming.

'What does it matter? I'll screw around, you'll screw your secretary, but don't worry, I'll not leave you. We need each other, we're a great team.'

Clare listened, not sure what to make of the conversation. With Harry, it had been one man, one woman, and fidelity, but here were the Dowlings, two people who were married and wanted to stay that way, yet they regarded fidelity as a dispensable commodity.

'Who else in this room have you slept with? You're the one with your night of truths. Then come out with it, tell all,' Len Dowling said. 'Who else have you screwed: Dennison, Jimmy, although he may be a little too young, even for you. I assume you draw the line somewhere, although Freestone could just about manage it. Certainly not Winston; he's only able to make it with men. Come on, who is it?'

Fiona realised that she was enjoying the argument, appreciative of an audience, oblivious of whether they approved of her or not. 'Okay, if you must know, I was sleeping with Bill Ford.'

Tremayne sat up at the revelation. 'Mrs Dowling, is that true?' he asked.

'It's true. The man was lonely, in need of a woman. He told me one night after rehearsals.'

'Not the night I found you screwing Geoff on the dining room floor,' Cheryl said.

'Not that night. I hope you had a good look,' Fiona said.

'There wasn't that much to see, other than Geoff's lily-white arse between your two legs, and your moaning. And besides, it's not the first time I've seen a man on top of you.'

Jimmy Francombe loved the spectacle; he knew he'd have plenty to tell his friends. The conversation, the visual images in his mind, were causing him to get an erection. He grabbed a magazine from a table close to where he was sitting and placed it over his lap.

'That night with Bill Ford, the three of us, is that it? You weren't looking so good that night either.'

'At least I don't pretend to be holier than thou. My past is an open book; I'm neither proud nor dismissive of it, and Gary knows all about it. And believe me, with Gary it will only be him and his children. I suppose it's because Len's such a lousy lay.'

'And you'd know, wouldn't you?'

'A long time ago, but yes, I know. I suppose the woman in his office, the dark-haired one, she'd be able to corroborate Len's lovemaking ability.'

The two women came at each other, or Fiona did, Cheryl responding. Clare stepped in and separated them. Jimmy Francombe was beside himself with excitement, Trevor Winston took in all that was occurring. Peter Freestone sat quietly, pleased that his daughter had severed her friendship with the women in her early teens. The Dennisons sat to one side, saying nothing.

Tremayne re-entered the fray, and Clare sat on a seat equidistant from the two women.

'Mrs Dowling, we were led to believe that you were fond of Geoff Pearson. If, as you have professed previously, you love your husband and were fond of Pearson, then why were you involved with Bill Ford?' Tremayne asked.

'He was a good man, a man that I loved in my rebellious teenage years.'

'Is that the reason?'

'The man was lonely, and in need of affection. We'd meet occasionally, that's all.'

'That's all?' Len Dowling said.

'Shut up, Len, you're becoming a bore,' Fiona said. 'You knew what I was when I married you. We're a team, but for tonight, this one night, I intend to reveal everything, the same as everyone else. I didn't kill Geoff, although I was angry with him, and I didn't kill Bill Ford for the one reason that I couldn't: the man was more important to me than that. And I didn't kill Gordon Mason.'

'But I could have killed Bill, and you've given them a motive,' Dowling said.

'Not you, you couldn't harm a fly,' Fiona said. 'You may be able to sell them a house, but that's as far as it goes.'

'Mr and Mrs Dowling, can we come back to Bill Ford. We know about your past relationship with the man, we know that you and Cheryl had a threesome.'

Jimmy Francombe excused himself and dashed to the bathroom. He looked at Cheryl as he left and smiled. She did not return the smile but continued to look at the woman who had angered her, although she knew it was not anger that would last. The woman, for all her faults, was still her friend.

'Mr Dowling, Len, your wife has given multiple motives for wanting Gordon Mason and Bill Ford dead,' Tremayne said. 'Are you willing to confess to their murders?'

'Why me? What about the others? Cheryl's been around, the same as Fiona. Why don't you ask her if she was screwing Ford as well? Or maybe Gary was jealous of a previous lover, wanted him dead. What if Cheryl was screwing Mason? Maybe he had something on her, something he didn't want Gary to know.'

Cheryl Milledge sat still, outwardly portraying calmness, inwardly seething. 'I was not involved with either of the two men. Gordon Mason was an awful man, Bill was not,' she said.

'Let me put this to you,' Tremayne said. 'If Bill Ford had approached you to admit that he was lonely, would you have slept with him?'

'Before I met Gary, I would have, but now, not a chance. As much as I liked Bill, there's no way that I would cheat on Gary, or him on me. Fiona, for all her airs and graces, has not changed; I have.'

Chapter 24

Clare had not said much so far. She felt the need to remind
Tremayne of the structure of the evening. 'Guv, we should ask
the others here to offer their opinions of what has happened so
far. Did Fiona kill Geoff Pearson out of passion and anger? Did
Len kill Mason and Ford? Or did someone else kill Ford?'

'I did not kill Geoff,' Fiona said. Clare noticed that she
was no longer holding her husband's hand and that they had
separated by at least a foot on the sofa they sat on.

'This is a murder mystery,' Clare said. 'All possibilities are
open to conjecture. We do not have fictitious deaths here, only
real ones with real killers.'

'Very well, carry on. Have your entertainment at my cost.'

'There is no entertainment here tonight,' Tremayne said
to the assembled participants. This is a murder enquiry, and
tonight, I can assure you, someone is going to be arrested for
murder. I don't know who, but I have my suspicions. It will be up
to all those present to assist Yarwood and myself in this matter.'

'And if we don't?' Phillip Dennison asked.

'Your non-compliance is an indication that you are hiding
something. There is a hidden component in this enquiry. We need
to find it.'

'Not with me there isn't,' Samantha Dennison said. 'I
married Phillip for his money, he married me as a reward. It's a
good arrangement, and we prefer to be together, not apart. As
for me, I've slept with enough men in my time. I do not need an
old and angry man who insulted me or someone who spent his
time with the dead.'

'What about Geoff Pearson?' Fiona asked. 'Were you
screwing him?'

'Not a chance. He tried it on, but I know which side my
bread is buttered. I have no intention of cheating on Phillip;
count me out as a potential murderer.'

'Before we move on to the others in this room, let us have everyone's opinion of Fiona and Len Dowling. A show of hands will be sufficient. As for the Dowlings, I would remind you that this is a police enquiry,' Tremayne said.

'I'll not stay here to be judged,' Len Dowling said.

'Listen to the detective inspector, Len. Inspector Tremayne is right. We're only guilty of offending public morality, not of killing someone. If the others in this room want to pass judgement, then so be it. I'll not object,' Fiona said.

'Did Fiona push Geoff Pearson,' Tremayne said, 'knowing full well that the drop was sufficient to cause him injury? Remember, death was not certain from the fall, in that the grass below was wet from the recent rain. It was soft underfoot. That does not obviate her intention to murder, just the fact that death could not be guaranteed. If he had not hit his head on the ruins' protruding stones on the way down, he might have broken some bones, but possibly nothing more.'

The hands went up around the room. Clare counted them. 'Mrs Dowling, it appears that the majority believe that you acted out of anger.'

'What about Cheryl? She didn't put her hand up,' Fiona said.

'I've known you longer than anyone else. You were angry, but you did not mean him any harm. You're innocent of that crime,' Cheryl said.

The two women stood up and hugged each other. 'You're a bitch, but you're still my friend,' Cheryl said.

Tremayne needed to wind up the heat; a tender moment between the two women had brought a sense of calm to the room. 'Let us come to Len Dowling, a man who has every right to dislike Mason and Ford. One was forcing his wife into sex, the other she has voluntarily admitted to sleeping with. What man would not be driven to murder?'

'If Len did kill Mason,' Freestone said, 'then he has my acceptance for what he did. I liked Bill Ford, even met up with him on occasions, yet the man is party to adultery. He was a man who had great respect in the community, yet the chance to sleep with Fiona and he took it.'

'He did not take it, I offered. He was my friend, and I cared for him.'

'It doesn't excuse him.'

'What man could resist? Bill was guilty of no crime, and he does not deserve your condemnation. I know all about you,' Fiona said.

'What do you know?' Clare asked.

'I know that he has used his influence as a city councillor to his advantage.'

'Is this about the land deal that we were investigating?'

'No, but he's used his influence elsewhere, the same as everyone on the council.'

'Cheryl, she works in the building department,' Tremayne said.

'She's not involved.'

'Can you prove what you've said against Peter Freestone?'

'It's not a crime, just unethical, that's all.'

'That's slanderous,' Freestone said. 'I've always acted in the best interests of the community.'

'Fiona, you've got a big mouth,' Len Dowling said. 'This is going to cause trouble.'

'Why? It's in here, not outside. The next question is whether you killed Mason and Bill. Is that correct, Detective Inspector?'

'Yes.'

'Thank you. What do you want, Len? Do you want Peter Freestone sitting there voting against you? I know he's a friend of the detective inspector. If you killed Mason, then admit it, even if you killed Bill, but don't allow yourself to be judged by anyone else in this room. They've all got things they'd rather keep hidden.'

'I don't,' Jimmy Francombe said.

'Too young, is that it?'

'I didn't kill anyone.'

'What about you and Trevor? Are you his playmate? You're always friendly.'

'That's scurrilous, and you know it,' Winston said. He had been enjoying the spectacle of the Dowlings sounding off at each other.

'Maybe it is, but what have you got to hide, Trevor?' Fiona said. 'What's hidden in your cupboard? You must be sleeping with someone, and if it's not Jimmy, then who is it? What is the dirt on you?'

'There is no dirt on me. I have some friends, but they're not here. I hated Gordon Mason, liked Bill, but I did not kill either of them.'

'And what about you two, Mr and Mrs Perfect?' Fiona said, focussing her interest on the Dennisons.

'You've got a foul mouth, Fiona,' Phillip Dennison said. 'What have we done to you? I've always been polite, never tried it on with you, not that I ever fancied you.'

'What do you mean? You prefer a painted tart to me, is that it? Does a mature woman intimidate you, or do you get your kicks with adolescent females?'

'I'm not an adolescent,' Samantha Dennison said. 'I'm over the age of consent and Phillip treats me well, more than can be said for your husband.'

'I've no complaints with Len, but look at you. Do you dress up in a school uniform for him: frilly knickers, a short skirt, tight blouse, pretend that he's your teacher about to give you a spanking. Is that how he gets his kicks?'

'You bitch,' Phillip Dennison said. 'Don't talk to my wife like that.'

'I know about you and your offshore companies, you fiddling the tax man.'

'How?'

'Chris has the dirt on you, the same as Freestone does. Is Peter Freestone to be the next man you kill? Did Gordon Mason know what you were?'

Tremayne felt the need to interject. 'Mr Dennison, you're obviously very successful. This raises the question as to whether your financial dealings, your business structure, are fully legal.'

'They are. Fiona and Len are just fishing, aiming to direct the blame away from Len. I have not broken any laws.'

Clare thought that Phillip Dennison had probably done nothing wrong, but she could not be sure. What was sure was that any group of people would have something they did not want to be revealed, even her, but she was not defending herself; the others were, and so far, no one had cracked, although some were wounded. Fiona was, as was her husband, but she was sure they would rise above it. For Freestone, the mere suggestion that he had not conducted his city councillor's duties in accordance with the guidelines would lead to him being ejected from the position. It was a motive for murder, and Mason was the sort of man who would reveal the wrongdoing, but what about Bill Ford? The man had no black marks against him, other than he had been sleeping with another man's wife.

Jimmy Francombe, apart from his overactive teenage hormones, seemed harmless, as did Trevor Winston. Both seemed the least likely, in that one was young, the other older and homosexual. Killing Mason may have had some validity for Winston, but not Bill Ford, who was known not to be gay.

'This is going nowhere,' Gary Barker said.

'The night's young,' Tremayne said.

'You can't hold us here against our will.'

'Outside there is a police car. Anyone who feels inclined to leave will be taken down to the police station for questioning. It's either here or down there, you can decide.'

'In that case, get on with it,' Freestone said.

'Let us examine the Dennisons,' Tremayne said.

'Why us?' Phillip Dennison asked. 'We're an open book.'

Clare decided it was time for her to speak. 'Not so long ago, Samantha was placed under control. I believe that you slapped her, took away her credit cards and the key to the Aston Martin. Is that correct?'

'Phillip was under a lot of strain,' Samantha said. She had her arm through her husband's.

'DI Tremayne and I have spoken to you on several occasions. I don't remember you defending your husband at those times.'

'I was wrong.'

'You said that you were the trophy, he was the older man, and if he could not keep you in the manner that you required, then you would leave, take your share of the assets, and find someone else.'

'That's what I said.'

'What has changed?'

'I don't want to leave Phillip. He's a good man, always treated me well.'

'Is it because you will not get your share of his money? What if he's found guilty of murder? How will that affect your wealth? You're the legal wife, and you'll have access to his money. I put it to you that you know he is guilty of murder and that you are waiting for him to be arrested. That is why we are so welcome here tonight. You just need one more night of pretence, and then this is all yours. Am I right?' Clare said. She realised that what she had just said was plausible.

'That's rubbish. Phillip knows that I want him here, not in prison.'

'How does he know? Did you twist him around your finger, flaunt the assets? Samantha, compared to you, Fiona Dowling is a paragon of virtue.'

'Don't compare me to that woman. She screws who she wants, I don't. I've got Phillip, I don't need anyone else. Her husband may be lousy in bed, but Phillip is not.'

'How did you know about my husband's lovemaking?' Fiona asked.

'You told me.'

'No, I didn't. Who have you been talking to? Bill Ford? Have you been screwing Len?'

'Why would I do that? I've no need of another man.'

***

The evening was going well; Tremayne sat back to let the
fireworks continue. So far, he kept coming back to Fiona
Dowling. Her husband, Len, had not acquitted himself any better
either, but loose morals, a lack of backbone, were not confessions
of guilt. The constant haranguing across the room had not, so
far, produced any indication of who he would be placing in
handcuffs before the end of the evening.

The tension between Samantha Dennison and Fiona
Dowling was palpable. Both women had dressed for the occasion.
Cheryl Milledge had arrived wearing a tee-shirt and a pair of
jeans. Clare could see that Cheryl and Gary Barker were hitting
the beer and were becoming drunk. She let them continue,
knowing that both could drink a lot, and tongues loosen with
alcohol. Fiona Dowling was steering clear of alcohol, as was
Samantha Dennison. Clare did not like Fiona any more than her
senior did, but Samantha had acquitted herself well. For a woman
who had had no involvement with the dramatic society except on
infrequent occasions, she seemed to know a lot about them,
especially Len Dowling and his inability to keep his wife from
straying.

'Samantha,' Clare said, 'you told me about your past once.
Are you willing to reveal it here?'

'What's there to tell. I was working in an office, being
accosted by every rampant male. One day in comes Phillip, we
start talking and then soon after we are married.'

'This is a night for warts and all. Why Phillip? Was it love
or his money?'

'His money initially, but after that love. Phillip treats me
well, I am content.'

'The need for a younger man must remain. My apologies
to your husband, but you're young and full of vitality, your
husband is at the age of slowing down.'

'I look as though I need a man constantly in my bed, but
that's not the case. I've enjoyed the ability to spend, to live well,
but there are times when I could stay at home and read a book.'

'Are you well read?'

'Yes, and well-educated.'

'Then you, as the only bystander here tonight, let us have your opinion as to who the murderer is.'

Samantha focussed on those assembled in that elegant room with its paintings on the wall, the flat-screen TV, the expensive furniture. 'There are three deaths,' Samantha commenced. 'Gordon Mason, Geoff Pearson, and Bill Ford.'

'I did not murder Geoff,' Fiona shouted. Clare looked over at her, holding a finger to her mouth in a gesture to be quiet and sit down.

'Let me deal with Gordon Mason,' Samantha continued. 'The man was an obnoxious bore. I did not like him, but his comments meant little to me. I know that is how most of you see me, a cheap slut selling herself to an older man, but you're too polite, or not committed enough, to say anything. Mason was, as you say, killed at Old Sarum, probably by two men. Neither Fiona nor Cheryl are involved. Those who killed him must have had a close relationship to consider such an option. Alternatively, there was one man with two daggers.'

'Impossible to swap in a frenzy,' Clare said.

'Then it was one man on the stage, another off the stage. Was the body visible at all times?'

'Yes, and he was dead by the time he was placed on the stretcher by Mark Antony.'

'Then it's two of the men on the stage, but which two? Phillip tends to be a loner, and not involved with the other men in the dramatic society. Len could be involved with Peter Freestone, complementary professions, and Gordon Mason would have been able to see through any crooked deals they had hatched together.'

Freestone made a move to open his mouth. Tremayne looked over at him, a clear sign to keep quiet and to let the woman talk.

'Geoff Pearson, from what I can see, had no reason to kill Mason, no collusion, no special relationship with anyone else in the group,' Samantha continued. 'The man was attracted to women, not men, and as we can see with Fiona, he was not averse to seducing Len's wife. He was a young man full of libido, and he must have had a great deal of satisfaction acting on that stage with Len, the unknowing husband. Geoff, for all his virtues, was a shallow man, bereft of true emotions, other than for self. He is not a murderer, but not a person of true substance either. Len, for all his faults, is. He's a man who stands by his wife, the most devious of all of us here tonight. The woman has not handled herself well, and those that she calls her friends, are not. They're fair weather, not visible when times are tough.'

'Not like me,' Cheryl said.

'Cheryl is a decent person, and, as she says, she is a true friend. The only one who was with Fiona when she was arrested after Geoff's death. However, I don't believe that Fiona wanted the man dead, although she would not have been upset to have seen him in the hospital. Regardless of what I've said, I don't see Fiona as a murderer.'

'Everyone will have their say after Mrs Dennison has finished,' Tremayne said.

'Gary Barker is a man who lets life pass him by, not interfering with its flow,' Samantha said. 'He's now got Cheryl to look after him. The two of them complement each other, and Gary could not kill anyone; it's not in his nature to take himself or life too seriously. Cheryl has a kind heart and the anger to kill Mason, but not the opportunity, and she would not have been capable of killing Bill Ford, a former lover, and still a friend of hers and Fiona.'

'What about the relationship between Peter Freestone and Len Dowling?' Tremayne asked. He had changed his opinion of Dennison's wife. Regardless of why she had married her husband, she was an articulate woman. He was willing to let her continue, although he had a shrewd idea where she was heading.

Samantha, emboldened by her new-found importance, stood up and moved to one corner of the room. 'Len would not be capable. He's able to run a successful business due to Fiona's support and pushing him on, but he could not kill anyone. Maybe if Fiona had pushed him hard enough, but she wouldn't. Not that she would have any issues with doing that, a good woman on your side in a fight, but her social prestige is all important to her. She's admitted to sleeping with Mason, and whereas she may say he's an odious man, it would have only been a case of lying on her back, opening her legs, and thinking of England, or whatever she thinks off. Probably her social standing, as that is more important. Apart from that, she'd have no reason to kill Mason. She is not a likeable person. Sorry, but there it is.'

Fiona Dowling sat in her chair, saying nothing. Tremayne looked over at her, could see the anger directed at Samantha Dennison. 'Mrs Dowling, I suggest you digest what Samantha has just said,' Tremayne said. 'Harsh words, but she's just given you the best alibi possible.'

'I don't like what she said,' Fiona replied.

'Maybe you don't, but we're here to solve a murder, not to make friends. After tonight, you can all go your separate ways, but for now, Mrs Dennison has the floor.'

Samantha continued. 'Len could not kill Mason without his wife's direction, and even if he had known about her and Bill Ford, he would have done nothing, or maybe remonstrated with the man, attempted to push him around, but that's all. The man does not have the backbone, I believe we're all agreed on that.'

Len and Fiona Dowling sat close to each other again, holding hands.

'And if Len and Peter were involved in something illegal and they wanted Mason dead, there's no way that Len would act without his wife's encouragement, which would then mean that Peter Freestone knew of Fiona in the background, and besides, Peter did not kill Mason.'

'That's correct,' Tremayne said. 'He had only one stab at Mason. If it was to be a murder, it has to be those who stabbed him more than once.'

'There are only two left,' Samantha said. 'Does anyone want to take over or shall I wrap up this night?'

'Carry on,' Clare said.

'You're doing a fine job,' Tremayne said. No one else said anything. Phillip Dennison looked at his wife in admiration.

Cheryl and Gary were no longer drinking. Trevor Winston and Jimmy Francombe sat motionlessly.

'Doesn't anyone else see it?' Samantha said.

'What do you mean?' Clare said.

'Jimmy, he's gay.'

'I'm not,' Jimmy protested.

'Let Mrs Dennison continue,' Tremayne said. 'Everyone else sat quietly while she was denouncing or exonerating them. You will do the same,' he said, directing his gaze at the young man.

'The over-attentiveness to women, the need to chat them up, to show off how manly he is in front of his friends. I've seen it before. I'm sure he's tried it on with Clare and Fiona.'

'He has with me,' Clare said.

'He got a smack from me for trying to look down my blouse,' Fiona said.

'Trevor Winston is gay. The two of them are lovers.'

'That's not fair. I'm straight,' Jimmy said.

'Let me put it to everyone here,' Samantha said. 'When has anyone here seen Jimmy with a woman? He's eighteen, the city of Salisbury is awash with teenage girls looking to be taken out. He's an attractive young man, and he'd have no trouble seducing a few, but where are they? Has he ever brought any to your rehearsals? He's a show-off, but he never shows a woman. The man is gay, and so is Trevor.'

'We've not seen him with a girlfriend,' Fiona said.

'Nor have I,' Cheryl said.

'Mrs Dennison, Samantha, please continue,' Tremayne said. 'And Trevor and Jimmy, please be quiet. Samantha has the floor, and we intend to hear her out.'

'But—' Jimmy started to say.

'You've heard the police officer,' Trevor said. 'Let Samantha have her say. You'll get a chance afterwards.'

'Trevor is openly gay and proud of it,' Samantha said, 'but he's a mature man in a liberated society. Jimmy is still concerned about how his friends see him, not willing to tell his parents either. There is only one conclusion.'

'Which is?' Tremayne asked. Everyone in the room was listening with bated breath. No one was eating or drinking.

'Trevor and Jimmy killed Gordon Mason.'

'And Bill Ford?' Clare asked.

'Mason knew about them. The man was vindictive enough, bigoted, willing to tell Jimmy's school friends that he was gay, as well as his parents. Neither he nor Trevor could allow that to occur.'

'It's a lie,' Trevor Winston said, jumping to his feet.

'Mr Winston, please sit down. You'll have a chance to offer a defence. Mrs Dennison, please continue,' Tremayne said.

'Bill Ford would not have been interested, and the man's discretion was well known. He knew about Fiona's and Cheryl's past histories, the fact that he had slept with both of them. The fact that Jimmy was gay and sleeping with Trevor would not have concerned him. He may have had a word in Jimmy's ear to tell him to be more careful, but he would have done no more. They killed Bill Ford, but not because he threatened their cosy love nest; they killed him because they enjoyed it.'

'Only one of them killed him,' Clare said.

'One dagger and the place was cleaned afterwards.'

'Spotlessly.'

'You've been to Trevor's hairdressing salon. How would you describe it?'

'Spotless.'

'Precisely. One of the two stabbed the man, the other was present, and may or may not have taken an active part.'

'It was Trevor's idea,' Jimmy Francombe said as he stood up and moved to the other side of the room.'

'Shut up, just shut up. They can't prove anything,' Trevor Winston shouted at him.

'I didn't want to kill Bill Ford. It was Trevor's idea.'

Clare went over and stood next to the young man. 'Why did you kill Bill Ford?' she asked.

'It was Trevor; he stabbed him. I wasn't in the room. Bill was a good man, my friend.'

'Yet you let the man be murdered. Why?'

'Trevor thought it would be fun, but I didn't.'

'Why Mason?' Clare asked. She looked over at Tremayne, saw him signalling out of the window for a couple of uniforms to come in.

'Gordon was going to tell my parents. I couldn't let him do that.'

'But why murder?'

'You don't understand. You're young and pretty. I hate being what I am, but I can't help it. Trevor knew what I was six months ago. He put pressure on me, I reacted.'

'Reacted?'

'Okay. I slept with him.'

'And how did that feel?'

'Dirty, but I couldn't stop. And then Gordon Mason was threatening to tell my parents if I didn't stop sleeping with Trevor.'

'How did he know?'

'He saw us once in Trevor's car after rehearsals. The man was nosy, that's how he knew about Geoff and Fiona. He observed, prowled around, probably a peeping tom as well, getting his kicks watching others screw.'

'Did he enjoy watching you and Trevor?'

'Maybe, maybe not. I don't know. Trevor said we had to kill him, make it look as if it was an accident.'

'And you agreed?'

'What could I do? I want to finish school, go to university, and now what?'

The others in the room said nothing. Fiona sat close to Len, Samantha near to her husband. Peter Freestone relaxed back in his chair. Tremayne was on his feet, as were the two uniforms who had entered through a door at the rear.

'You damn fool,' Trevor Winston said. 'If you had only kept quiet.'

'Mr Winston, why did you kill Bill Ford?'

'Jimmy did, not me.'

'You liar, you bloody liar. You enjoyed every moment up there at Old Sarum.'

'Mr Francombe, are you willing to confess to the murder of Gordon Mason?' Tremayne asked.

'Yes, but I did not kill Bill Ford. I liked the man.'

'You've said that already,' Tremayne said. 'You will be taken from here and formally charged with murder.'

'What will happen?'

'That depends on a judge and jury, not me. Yarwood, can you accompany Francombe to the police station, let his parents know?'

'I'll do it,' Clare said.

Tremayne turned to Trevor Winston. 'You will be charged with the murders of Gordon Mason and Bill Ford. Do you have anything to say?'

'You can't prove it.'

'Jimmy Francombe is young. He'll get off with a shortened sentence due to his youth. As long as he maintains his story, he'll be out in a few years. You, Mr Winston, will not. The only hope you will have is to plead guilty, hopeful of a reduced sentence due to insanity.'

'They'll not believe me,' Winston said.

'Killing a man just because you enjoy the thrill of it is hardly the act of a sane man.'

'You may be right. I'll take legal advice first.'

'That's your prerogative. Mine is to arrest you for the murders of Gordon Mason and Bill Ford,' Tremayne said. 'Take him away,' he said to one of the uniforms.

Clare left with Jimmy Francombe, Tremayne returned to his seat. 'A successful evening,' he said.

'Successful, is that how you'd describe it?' Peter Freestone said.

'I'm sorry for what has been said here tonight, but it was necessary. Murder is a crime that brings out the worst in people, that makes emotions raw. Hopefully, you can all forgive what was said, what was revealed.'

'I can,' Fiona Dowling said. 'Trevor would not have stopped. He'd have chosen another target, any one of us.'

'Thank you,' Cheryl Milledge said. Samantha Dennison came over and gave Tremayne a kiss on the cheek. The DI sat back, complacent, knowing full well that it would take a week to wrap up the paperwork, and then it was a holiday in Spain with Jean, his former wife. He had to admit that he was looking forward to it.

The End

ALSO BY THE AUTHOR

Murder is the Only Option – A DCI Cook Thriller

A man, thought to be long dead, returns to exact revenge against those who had blighted his life. His only concern is to protect his wife and daughter. He will stop at nothing to achieve his aim.

'Big Greg, I never expected to see you around here at this time of night.'

'I've told you enough times.'

'I've no idea what you're talking about,' Robertson replied. He looked up at the man, only to see a metal pole coming down at him. Robertson fell down, cracking his head against a concrete kerb.

The two vagrants, no more than twenty feet away, did not stir and did not even look in the direction of the noise. If they had, they would have seen a dead body, another man walking away.

Death Unholy – A DI Tremayne Thriller

All that remained were the man's two legs and a chair full of greasy and fetid ash. Little did DI Keith Tremayne know that it was the beginning of a journey into the murky world of paganism and its ancient rituals. And it was going to get very dangerous.

'Do you believe in spontaneous human combustion?' Detective Inspector Keith Tremayne asked.

'Not me. I've read about it. Who hasn't?' Sergeant Clare Yarwood answered.

I haven't,' Tremayne replied, which did not surprise his young sergeant. In the months they had been working together, she had come to realise that he was a man who had little interest in the world. When he had a cigarette in his mouth, a beer in his hand, and a murder to solve he was about the happiest she ever saw him. He could hardly be regarded as one of life's sociable people. And as for reading? The most he managed was an occasional police report or an early morning newspaper, turning first to the back pages for the racing results.

Murder in Little Venice – A DCI Cook Thriller

A dismembered corpse floats in the canal in Little Venice, an upmarket tourist haven in London. Its identity is unknown, but what is its significance?

DCI Isaac Cook is baffled about why it's there. Is it gang-related, or is it something more?

Whatever the reason, it's clearly a warning, and Isaac and his team are sure it's not the last body that they'll have to deal with.

Murder is only a Number – A DCI Cook Thriller

Before she left she carved a number in blood on his chest. But why the number 2, if this was her first murder?

The woman prowls the streets of London. Her targets are men who have wronged her. Or have they? And why is she keeping count?

DCI Cook and his team finally know who she is, but not before she's murdered four men. The whole team are looking for her, but the woman keeps disappearing in plain sight. The pressure's on to stop her, but she's always one step ahead.

And this time, DCS Goddard can't protect his protégé, Isaac Cook, from the wrath of the new commissioner at the Met.

Murder House – A DCI Cook Thriller

A corpse in the fireplace of an old house. It's been there for thirty years, but who is it?

It's clearly murder, but who is the victim and what connection does the body have to the previous owners of the house. What is the motive? And why is the body in a fireplace? It was bound to be discovered eventually but was that what the murderer wanted? The main suspects are all old and dying, or already dead.

Isaac Cook and his team have their work cut out trying to put the pieces together. Those who know are not talking because of an old-fashioned belief that a family's dirty laundry should not be aired in public, and certainly not to a policeman – even if that means the murderer is never brought to justice!

Murder is a Tricky Business – A DCI Cook Thriller

A television actress is missing, and DCI Isaac Cook, the Senior Investigation Officer of the Murder Investigation Team at Challis Street Police Station in London, is searching for her.

Why has he been taken away from more important crimes to search for the woman? It's not the first time she's gone missing, so why does everyone assume she's been murdered?

There's a secret, that much is certain, but who knows it? The missing woman? The executive producer? His eavesdropping assistant? Or the actor who portrayed her fictional brother in the TV soap opera?

Murder Without Reason – A DCI Cook Thriller

DCI Cook faces his greatest challenge. The Islamic State is waging war in England, and they are winning.

Not only does Isaac Cook have to contend with finding the perpetrators, but he is also being forced to commit actions contrary to his mandate as a police officer.

And then there is Anne Argento, the prime minister's deputy. The prime minister has shown himself to be a pacifist and is not up to the task. She needs to take his job if the country is to fight back against the Islamists.

Vane and Martin have provided the solution. Will DCI Cook and Anne Argento be willing to follow it through? Are they able to act for the good of England, knowing that a criminal and murderous action is about to take place? Do they have any option?

The Haberman Virus

A remote and isolated village in the Hindu Kush mountain range in North Eastern Afghanistan is wiped out by a virus unlike any seen before.

A mysterious visitor clad in a space suit checks his handiwork, a female American doctor succumbs to the disease, and the woman sent to trap the person responsible falls in love with him – the man who would cause the deaths of millions.

Hostage of Islam

Three are to die at the Mission in Nigeria: the pastor and his wife in a blazing chapel; another gunned down while trying to defend them from the Islamist fighters.

Kate McDonald, an American, grieving over her boyfriend's death and Helen Campbell, whose life had been troubled by drugs and prostitution, are taken by the attackers.

Kate is sold to a slave trader who intends to sell her virginity to an Arab Prince. Helen, to ensure their survival, gives herself to the murderer of her friends.

Malika's Revenge

Malika, a drug-addicted prostitute, waits in a smugglers' village for the next Afghan tribesman or Tajik gangster to pay her price, a few scraps of heroin.

Yusup Baroyev, a drug lord, enjoys a lifestyle many would envy. An Afghan warlord sees the resurgence of the Taliban. A Russian white-collar criminal portrays himself as a good and honest citizen in Moscow.

All of them are linked in an audacious plan to increase the quantity of heroin shipped out of Afghanistan and into Russia and ultimately the West.

Some will succeed, some will die, some will be rescued from their plight and others will rue the day they became involved.

ABOUT THE AUTHOR

Phillip Strang was born in England in the late forties, during the post-war baby boom. He had a comfortable middle-class upbringing, spending his childhood years in a small town seventy miles west of London.

His childhood and the formative years were a time of innocence. There were relatively few rules, and as a teenager he had complete freedom, thanks to a bicycle – a three-speed Raleigh. It was in the days before mobile phones, the internet, terrorism and wanton violence. He was an avid reader of science fiction in his teenage years: Isaac Asimov, Frank Herbert, the masters of the genre. Much of what they and others mentioned has now become a reality. Science fiction has now become science fact. Still an avid reader, the author now mainly reads thrillers.

In his early twenties, the author, with a degree in electronics engineering and a desire to see the world, left the cold, damp climes of England for Sydney, Australia – his first semi-circulation of the globe. Now, forty years later, he still resides in Australia, although many intervening years were spent in a myriad of countries, some calm and safe, others no more than war zones.

Printed in Great Britain
by Amazon